THE DEVIL'S CHURCH AND OTHER STORIES

cp cloth 12⁵⁰

pb - 25⁰⁰

THE DEVIL'S CHURCH

AND OTHER STORIES

BY MACHADO DE ASSIS

TRANSLATED BY JACK SCHMITT

AND LORIE ISHIMATSU

UNIVERSITY OF TEXAS PRESS   AUSTIN & LONDON

The Texas Pan American Series
is published with the assistance of a
revolving publication fund established by
the Pan American Sulphur Company.

Library of Congress Cataloging in Publication Data
Machado de Assis, Joaquim Maria, 1839–1908.
The Devil's Church and other stories.

(The Texas Pan American series)
CONTENTS: The Bonzo's Secret.—Those Cousins from
Sapucaia.—Alexandrian Tale.—The Devil's Church. [etc.]
I. Title.
PZ3.M1817De3 [PQ9697.M18]   869'.3   76-53828
ISBN 0-292-77535-0

Set in Korinna by G & S Typesetters Inc.

Printed in the United States of America

Illustrations on pages 28, 68, and 97 from Bettmann Archive.

CONTENTS

INTRODUCTION

The modern Brazilian short story begins with the mature works of Joaquim Maria Machado de Assis (1839–1908), acclaimed almost unanimously as Brazil's greatest writer. Between 1858 and 1906, Machado wrote more than two hundred stories, and no other writer in Brazil achieved his technical mastery of the story form before the 1930s.

Until recent years, Machado's reputation abroad was not commensurate with the quality of his remarkable stories and novels or his high position in Western letters. The Brazilian critic Antônio Cândido considered it a paradox that a writer of international stature, whose style and themes are characteristic of the twentieth century, should have remained relatively unknown outside Brazil. The obscurity of Machado's works in the United States was closely related to the fact that Portuguese was not widely known in this country, and translations of his novels and stories into English have been available only in recent years, thanks especially to the excellent translations by Helen Caldwell and William L. Grossman.

To our knowledge, only seventeen of Machado's short stories had appeared in English translation before the preparation of this collection. Three of those stories were anthologized by Isaac Goldberg in *Brazilian Tales* (1921). One of our stories—"The Companion" ("O Enfermeiro") —was published in Goldberg's book under the title of "The Attendant's Confession." Caldwell and Grossman translated twelve of Machado's best stories and had them published in *The Psychiatrist and Other Stories* (1963). They also published separately translations of "A Igreja do Diabo" and "Conto Alexandrino," which we have translated in the present volume under the titles of "The Devil's Church" and "Alexandrian Tale," respectively. In all, sixteen of our stories have never before appeared in English translation. We believe that all our stories, taken collectively, are representative of Machado's unique style and world view.

Machado's fiction can be divided roughly into two periods: those works written before and those written after 1880. The early Machado is basically romantic, whereas his late works are written in the vein of psychological realism. The Brazilian writer Augusto Meyer supports this division, comparing Machado's break in evolutionary continuity to that between Herman Melville's earlier works and *Moby-Dick*. Meyer's parallel is certainly valid. There is little in Machado's early novels and stories to prepare the reader for the abrupt changes in content and technique found in *Epitaph of a Small Winner* (*Memórias Póstumas de Brás Cubas*, 1880), his first great novel, and *Miscellaneous Papers* (*Papéis Avulsos*, 1882), the first of five volumes in which the majority of his best stories appear. The consistently high quality of the sixty-three narratives in these five books defies comparison with the works of other Brazilian short-story writers, past or present.

Machado's stories constitute an excellent satirical portrait of middle-class values and social structures in Brazil during the period of the Second Empire (1840–1890) and the first years of the Republic. If he had continued to publish the bland, moralistic love stories and parlor intrigues of the 1860s and 70s, his legacy to posterity would have been a mildly ironic but pleasant and entertaining portrait of a miniature *Belle Epoque* in a Brazilian setting. By the late 1870s, however, his fiction begins to reveal a devastatingly penetrating satirical assault on that society in particular and on humanity in general. In a moment of understatement, Helen Caldwell said that "one does not find in his writings a great deal of smug satisfaction with his own century and country."[1]

There is an abundance of implicit social criticism in Machado's descriptions of the life styles and the family structures of middle-class characters in his stories. One is always aware that the material comforts his characters enjoy are either the fruits of a carefully observed caste system or achieved at the expense of others: friendships and marriages are based on self-interest, financial position, or social class; government jobs and sinecures are arranged through close ties within the extended families of those who are actually forced to work for a living; upper-middle-class characters come by their leisure through inheritances, rents, or allowances from family estates; family retainers and impoverished relatives live out their lives as parasites or dependents. The sharpening of sadistic instincts and the avoidance of manual labor are possible results of the corrupting force of slavery. Many of Machado's characters seem to have a knack for avoiding useful work; they are idle, bored, passive, indifferent, and unresourceful, to the extent that they are often paralyzed when faced with the trauma of real action. The women in his stories are usually more social than domestic; they are vain, devoid of maternal instincts, and either physically, intellectually, or emotionally sterile.

We can see in Machado's critique of society that he prefers to dwell on

1. Helen Caldwell, *The Brazilian Othello of Machado de Assis* (Berkeley & Los Angeles: University of California Press, 1960).

the negative aspects of human behavior: egotism, pretentiousness, shallowness, corrosive envy and jealousy, cowardice, and intellectual lethargy. The more desirable qualities, such as philanthropy and altruism, are usually motivated by the less desirable ones.

Skeptical that the successes of science in the nineteenth century could be repeated in the areas of human values and behavior, Machado also doubts that the future has better things in store for us than the past. He is merciless in his satirization of intellectuals and scientists who offer dogmatically stated panaceas for the ills and shortcomings of humanity.

Machado's critique of literary conventions in Brazil is equally cutting. In his early literary essays and journalistic sketches, he offers constructive criticism, arguing persuasively against the Brazilian writers' emphasis on nature, the Indian, and the picturesque or exotic aspects of regionalism. After the mid-1870s, he begins to structure his critique of literary conventions within the fabric of his fiction, insulting his readers' traditional narrative expectations, satirizing romantic literary canons, and assaulting empty rhetoric, verbosity, and banality through the unimaginative flat language of his characters.

Although most of the human frailties Machado satirizes are not restricted to time and place—and are thus universal—many Brazilians have taken offense at his ironic barbs, accusing him of having painted an overly pessimistic portrait of Brazilian society, even denying him literary citizenship in Brazil.

Machado does in fact reveal sympathy for many of his characters, but it is an ironic sympathy. He is not indifferent to human conflicts, but he does use humor and irony to stress the absurdity and futility of those conflicts when acted out against the backdrop of a serene universe. Such a spectacle creates a sense of helplessness and can only inspire wistful amusement. The irony-laden controversies and reversals in his stories are intellectually satisfying and speculatively responsible; the staunch aesthetic moralism revealed in his narratives refutes those who consider his skepticism and pessimism nihilistic or sterile. It is not destructive to emphasize the presence of evil, the illusory nature of truth and reality, or the quagmires upon which people build the foundations of their speculative castles.

Many of Machado's best critics have hinted that his deepest meanings are found in his technique. Augusto Meyer claimed that the analysis of themes is a useless approach with Machado and concluded that ambiguity is the predominant theme in his works. As early as 1922, the American critic Isaac Goldberg saw that "we must not hunt too eagerly for action in

[Machado's] stories"; he is "sui generis, a literary law unto himself," and "his method is the most leisurely of indirection."[2] Years later, in 1948, Samuel Putnam recognized Machado's universal appeal and modernity and established a list of priorities for prospective readers and translators. Putnam also drew some valid parallels between Machado and Henry James: they both "deal in ideas" and are "concerned with psychological analysis, with the nebulous action that takes place behind the curtained consciousness of men"; they resemble one another in the "comparative absence of plot in their pages," as this term is commonly understood.[3] More recently, Caldwell posed the problem of ambiguity in Machado's works when she said that his leaving the reader to pass judgment is "to be sought in Machado's artistic method."[4]

As a result of his aversion to the superficiality of his contemporaries' interpretation of Brazilian reality, Machado attempts to portray a less idealized and more complex notion of human behavior. He strips his characters of their deceiving surface behavior and probes beyond their lives of public conformity. By aiming at psychological truth and focusing on crucial moments of experience in the lives of his characters, he approaches the method of the moderns. His ambiguity is in part the result of his subjective, relativistic world view, in which truth and reality, which are never absolutes, can only be approximated; no character relationships are stable, no issues are clear-cut, and the nature of everything is tenuous.

By exploring the subjective musings and the illusions of his characters, Machado leaves us no rational measure by which we may judge the flow of time, expanded and contracted at will in the individual consciousness of his characters. We attempt to make sense out of our experience, but our time sense is always relative to our perception of time at any given moment. In the words of A. A. Mendilow, the sensation of openness and expansion is further aided by the fact that "feelings and associations do not come to an end; they are not felt once and then finished with; they are not amenable to arrangement in shapes."[5] These "feelings and associations" are often the most tangible elements in Machado's better stories.

Barreto Filho makes an acute observation when he remarks that in Machado's narratives "there is a final conclusion of impotence, and that's why the evocation of the past is ironic."[6] This evocation of the past is ironic in Machado because despite our tendency to aspire to eternity, practice

2. Isaac Goldberg, *Brazilian Literature* (New York: Alfred A. Knopf, 1922).
3. Samuel Putnam, *Marvelous Journey* (New York: Farrar, Straus & Giroux, 1971).
4. Caldwell, *The Brazilian Othello*.
5. A. A. Mendilow, *Time and the Novel* (Deventer: Isel Press, 1952).
6. Barreto Filho, *Introdução a Machado de Assis* (Rio: Livraria Agir Editôra, 1947).

self-deception, and play mental games with time to make it serve ephemeral illusions, time is in fact a cross to bear; it passes on inexorably and remorselessly, destroying everything in its wake, save art and works of the intellect. Machado's experimentation with the time element is yet another facet of his fiction that gives his readers the distinct impression of modernity.

By communicating his meanings through the use of suggestion and implication, Machado developed a shorthand style that allowed him to convey progressively more information in smaller spaces. Sean O'Faolain stresses the modern writer's aim at "general revelation by suggestion" and "making a very tiny part do for a whole."[7] Machado, like the modern storyteller, "has not dispensed with incident or anecdote or plot and all their concomitants, but he *has* changed their nature. There is still adventure, but it is less a nervous suspense than an emotional or intellectual suspense."[8]

In his technical mastery of the short story, Machado was decades ahead of his contemporaries and can still be considered more modern than most of the modernists themselves. He is also an obligatory point of reference for anybody interested in the development of modern Brazilian literature. The fact that his works elicit extensive and diverse reactions and opinions is a tribute to the richness, complexity, and importance of those works.

Jack Schmitt
Lorie Ishimatsu

7. Sean O'Faolain, *The Short Story* (New York: Devin-Adair, 1964).
8. Ibid.

THE DEVIL'S CHURCH AND OTHER STORIES

THE BONZO'S SECRET

Unpublished Chapter by Fernão Mendes Pinto

I have just related the account of what happened to the very reverend Father Francisco in the city of Fuchéu, capital of the Kingdom of Bungo, and of how our Catholic King fared in the encounter between Father Francisco and the Fucarandono and other bonzos who disputed the primacy of our holy Roman Catholic religion. I shall now speak of a doctrine no less curious than beneficial to the soul, worthy of being made known throughout the republics of Christendom.

One day in the year of Our Lord 1552, as Diogo Meireles and I were strolling through the aforementioned city of Fuchéu, we came upon a group of people on a street corner, gathered around a native of that land who was engaged in a discourse punctuated with gestures and shouts. The crowd consisted solely of men, at least a hundred, all of whom stood gaping in awe at the speaker. Diogo Meireles, who knew the language better than I did because he'd spent many months in Bungo on a trade

Note: Bonzo ("Buddhist priest") also translates as "hypocrite" and "solemn" in Portuguese. "The Bonzo's Secret" is presented as an unpublished chapter of Mendes Pinto's famous *Peregrinação (Pilgrimage)*, an informative, antiheroic, and satirical account of Portuguese overseas expansion in Asia.—Trans.

mission (later, after having taken the appropriate studies, he distinguished himself in the practice of medicine), translated the speaker's words into our language. The speaker's main idea was that his only mission was to reveal the origin of crickets, which were born of the air or in the leaves of coconut palms during the conjunction of the new moon, and that his work, an impossible undertaking for anyone who was not a mathematician, physicist, and philosopher like himself, represented the fruit of long years of diligent experimentation, study, even danger to life and limb. But he had finally accomplished his goal, and the results of his labors brought glory to the Kingdom of Bungo, especially to the city of Fuchéu, of which he was a native son, and so certain was he that science was more valuable than the pleasures of life that he'd have accepted death on the spot if such a sacrifice were necessary. As soon as he had finished, the multitudes raised a deafening tumult of acclamation and carried the man off on their shoulders, shouting: "Patimau, Patimau, long live Patimau, who discovered the origin of crickets!" And they took him to the covered veranda of a merchant's stall, where they gave him refreshments and rendered him honor in the manner of those extremely accommodating and courteous heathens.

We were retracing our steps and discussing the singular discovery of the origin of crickets, when at a distance of no more than six *credos* from the merchant's veranda, we came upon yet another multitude gathered on a street corner, listening to another man. We were astonished by the similarity of the two situations, and since this man also spoke rapidly Diogo Meireles repeated the gist of his speech to me, as he had done before. To the great admiration and applause of those who surrounded him, this man—whose name was Languru—said that for those interested in salvation after the complete destruction of the earth, he had discovered the principle of afterlife in a single drop of cow's blood. His theory also explained the high esteem in which the cow was held as a habitation for human souls and the ardor with which that sacred animal was sought by men at the hour of their death. He had complete faith in the validity of his discovery, which was the result of continuous experimentation and profound cogitation, and he neither asked for nor wanted any recompense for his labors, other than glorifying the Kingdom of Bungo and receiving from it the esteem its honorable children deserved. The crowd, which had listened to his speech with great veneration, raised a tremendous outcry and took him off to the same merchant's veranda, with the difference that he was transported to it in a litter. When he arrived, he was showered with attentions and favors similar to those given to Patimau; in each instance, the foremost intention of the hosting multitudes was to express their gratitude to their honored guests. Since it seemed unlikely that the similarity between the two incidents was accidental, we didn't know what to make of it, and we didn't think that either of the theories—the origin of crickets revealed by Patimau or the principle of afterlife discovered by Languru— was rational or credible. At the time, we happened to be near the home of a sandalmaker named Titané, who rushed out to meet Diogo Meireles. As the two friends greeted one another, the sandalmaker addressed Diogo Meireles in the most lofty terms, calling him such things as "the voice of golden truth" and "the glorious lamp of thought." Diogo Meireles described what we had witnessed a short time before, and Titané responded excitedly, "Perhaps they're practicing a new doctrine, which is said to have been created by a bonzo of great learning who dwells on the slopes of Mount Coral." Since we expressed a burning desire to know more about the doctrine, Titané agreed to accompany us to the bonzo's domicile. He informed us that the bonzo opened his heart only to those who fervently desired to become adherents to his beliefs—we should thus pretend we were eager devotees to get him to tell us his doctrine, and if we liked it, we could put it into practice.

As planned, we went the following day to the home of the ancient bonzo Pomada,[1] who was one hundred and eight years old. He was exceedingly well versed in divine and human letters, and inasmuch as he was greatly revered by the peoples of that heathen nation, he was highly distrusted by the other bonzos, who were green with envy. And after Pomada learned through Titané who we were and what we wanted, he prepared us for the reception of his doctrine by performing various pagan ceremonies and rituals, then he raised his voice to divulge and explain his beliefs.

"You must understand," he began, "that virtue and knowledge have two parallel lives: first, in the person who possesses these qualities and, second, in the person who observes him. If you placed the most sublime virtues and profound knowledge in an individual who lived in a remote place, isolated from all contact with his fellow men, it would be as if he had no virtues or knowledge. If no one tastes it, an orange has no more value than heather or weeds, and if no one sees the orange, it is worthless. Stated another way, there is no spectacle without a spectator. One day, as I was pondering these matters, I realized I had spent my life trying to enlighten myself a little and without the presence of other men to see and honor me, my efforts would have been of no earthly use. Then I wondered if there was a way to receive the same consideration and honors without the expenditure of effort. I can now say that the day I discovered my doctrine was a day of regeneration and deliverance for mankind."

1. "Charlatan."—Trans.

At this point we were all ears, and our eyes were focused on the bonzo, who spoke slowly and clearly so I wouldn't miss a word, since Diogo Meireles had informed him that I wasn't familiar with the language of the land. And he said that the idea behind his new doctrine, which we could never have guessed on our own, had been inspired by nothing less than the celebrated moonstone, which was so dazzling that when placed on the peak of a mountain or the pinnacle of a tower, it illuminated even the most distant of the surrounding fields. The glittering moonstone didn't really exist, but many people believed it did, and more than one had claimed he had seen it with his own eyes. Then the bonzo said, "I considered the case and realized that if something can exist in opinion without existing in reality, or exist in reality without existing in opinion, the conclusion is that of the two parallel lives only opinion is necessary—not reality, which is only a secondary consideration. As soon as I made this speculative discovery, I thanked God for the special favor and decided to test the validity of my doctrine in experiments that have, in more than one instance, proven its soundness. But I won't go into that now, because I don't want to take any more of your time. In order to give you an understanding of my doctrine, it suffices to call your attention to the fact that, in the first place, crickets aren't born of the air or in the leaves of coconut palms during the conjunction of the new moon; second, the principle of afterlife can't be found in a single drop of cow's blood. But Patimau and Languru were so astute and managed to insinuate these ideas into the minds of the masses with such skill that they now enjoy the reputation of great physicists and greater philosophers, and they have followers who would sacrifice their lives for them."

We didn't know how best to express to the bonzo our feelings of extreme satisfaction and admiration. For some time thereafter, he continued to question us at great length about the fundamentals of his doctrine. When he was satisfied that we understood it, he cautioned us to practice and divulge it with discretion, not because there was anything in it that conflicted with divine or human laws but because misapplication by a neophyte could do it harm and ruin its chances of success. He finally bade us farewell and said he was certain we were leaving his home with the "true souls of pomadists," a denomination which pleased him to the extreme, as it was derived from his own name.

In fact, before nightfall the three of us had agreed to put to work an idea that seemed lucrative as well as judicious, since profit is found in the form not only of currency but also of esteem and praise, which are other means of exchange—even if we can't use them to buy damask fabrics or gold plate. Then in order to test the validity of the doctrine, each of us decided to instill in the minds of the citizens of Fuchéu a conviction which would allow us to enjoy benefits similar to those enjoyed by Patimau and Languru. As the saying goes, an individual's own best interests are usually uppermost in his mind, and Titané devised a scheme to receive payment in both currencies—hard cash and the esteem of his countrymen—by using the doctrine as a means of selling his sandals. We didn't oppose his idea since it didn't conflict with the essence of our doctrine.

I don't quite know how to explain Titané's experiment or make it understandable. In the Kingdom of Bungo, as in other remote areas of this part of the globe, the inhabitants make a high-quality paper from ground and gummed cinnamon bark, which is cut into pieces two palms long and half a palm wide. In vivid colors, the weekly news is printed on this paper in the language of the country—they write about politics, religion, business, the new laws of the kingdom, the arrival and departure of lateen- and balloon-rigged vessels, lancharas, spinnakers, and all the other kinds of ships that sail these seas, either waging war, which is frequent, or plying their trade. Every week great quantities of these news sheets are printed and distributed among the natives of the country for a gratuity, which each pays willingly so he may receive the paper before his neighbor. Titané found the perfect calling card in this paper, which in our language translates as "Lifeblood and Beacon of Mundane and Celestial Affairs." Although somewhat ornate, the title is suggestive. Titané had it printed in this paper that his sandals, according to the most recent news from the coasts of Malabar and China, were the talk of the day. In craftsmanship and style they were considered the best sandals in the world. At least twenty-two mandarins were petitioning the Celestial Emperor to honor them with the title of "Sandals of the Empire," and they were to be given by the Emperor as recompense to those who distinguished themselves in intellectual endeavors. Titané was doing his utmost to meet the ever-swelling demand for his product, not so much for love of profit as to bring honor to his country. But despite the demand for his sandals, he had informed the King that he was going to donate five hundred pairs of sandals to the poor. The fact that his sandals were considered the best in the world hadn't gone to his head, for he was still a humble craftsman, working for the glory of the Kingdom of Bungo. Until this time, people had considered his sandals adequate, but after reading the news they began to look for them with curiosity and enthusiasm, which increased with time, as Titané continued to seduce them with many extraordinary stories about his merchandise. With a professional air, he told us: "You can see I'm obeying the spirit of our doctrine, because I don't really believe in the superiority of my sandals, which are in fact mediocre. But I made the masses believe in them, and they're paying my price for them." Taking issue with him, I said, "I don't think you've captured the true meaning of our doctrine. We aren't supposed to instill in others an opinion that isn't ours, but rather make them believe we *can* do something we *can't* do. That's the essence of it."

Then they agreed it was my turn. I began at once, but I shall merely summarize my experiment and get on with the account of Diogo Meireles', as it was the most decisive of the three and offered the best proof of the effectiveness of the bonzo's delightful invention. I shall say only that since I knew a little about music and the shawm, which I didn't play very well, I decided to invite the most important citizens of Fuchéu to hear me play that instrument. They came, listened, and went away saying they had never heard anything so extraordinary. I confess that my success was due entirely to my manner of presentation: the graceful bending of my arms to pick up the shawm, which was brought to me on a silver tray, my proud and stiff posture, the unction with which I raised my eyes skyward and the disdainful pride with which I lowered them again to look at the crowd. At that point there broke out such a concert of enthusiastic outcries and applause that I was almost convinced that I merited this response.

But as I have already stated, Diogo Meireles' experiment was the most ingenious of all. At the time, there was a strange disease spreading throughout the city which made the victim's nose puff up until it covered more than half his face. In addition to looking dreadful, the afflicted had to put up with the inconvenience of carrying the extra weight. The physicians of the country proposed removing the swollen noses to relieve and cure the sick, but no one was willing to lend himself to this remedy, preferring excess to absence and considering removal the worst possible solution. More than one in this terrible predicament willingly died rather than be cured, and there was great sadness throughout the city of Fuchéu. As stated earlier, Diogo Meireles had been practicing medicine for some time. He studied the malady and concluded that disjoining the nose had two advantages: it could be accomplished without danger to the patient, and in the end he was no uglier than before, since no nose at all was no worse than a diseased, deformed, and heavy nose. But he was unable to persuade the unfortunate wretches to make the sacrifice. It was then that he happened upon his cunning invention. At a gathering of physicians, philosophers, bonzos, and other authorities and representatives of the community, he informed the assembly that he had devised a secret way to solve the problem by replacing the diseased organ with a healthy metaphysical nose, which—although it couldn't be perceived by human beings—was just as real or more real than the nose which had been removed. He had practiced this cure elsewhere, and it was highly accepted by the physicians of Malabar. Those assembled were astonished. Many reacted in disbelief, but the majority didn't know what to think. Although they abhorred the thought of a metaphysical nose, they were nonetheless seduced by the forcefulness of Diogo Meireles' lofty words and the conviction with which he expounded upon and defined his cure. A number of philosophers in attendance, somewhat embarrassed by Diogo Meireles' learned presentation and reluctant to give the impression that they knew less than he, declared that the foundations of his experiment were on solid ground in view of the fact that man was only the product of transcendental idealism. As a consequence, they claimed that there was more than sufficient reason to believe in metaphysical noses and swore that they were every bit as good as the other kind.

The assembly applauded Diogo Meireles. The diseased went to him in such great throngs that he had to devote all his energies to curing them. After skillfully removing a patient's nose, he would carefully dip his fingers into a box of metaphysical noses, take one out, and apply it to the empty spot. His patients, cured and compensated for their loss in this manner, looked at one another and could see nothing in the place of the organ that had been cut off. But they were so certain that the substitute organ was there—even though they couldn't see or feel it—that they didn't consider themselves cheated and went about their affairs.

The best proof of the doctrine and the success of Diogo Meireles' experiment is the fact that those who had had their noses cut off continued to use their handkerchiefs to blow them. I have related this tale in its entirety so that I might do honor to the bonzo and serve the interests of mankind.

THOSE COUSINS FROM SAPUCAIA

There are those elusive moments when an inopportune stroke of fate inflicts upon us two or three cousins from Sapucaia. At other times, on the contrary, these cousins from Sapucaia are more a blessing than a curse.

It all began at the door of a church. I was waiting for my cousins Claudina and Rosa to take their holy water so I could show them the way to our house, where they were staying. They had come from Sapucaia for Carnival, and they lingered two months in Rio. It was I who accompanied them everywhere—mass, the theater, Ouvidor Street—because my mother, with her rheumatism, could barely move about indoors, and they were not accustomed to going out by themselves. Sapucaia was our common homeland. Although our relatives were scattered throughout the country, it was there that the trunk of the family tree was born. My uncle José Ribeiro, father of these cousins, was the only one of five brothers to stay there, farming the land and involving himself in local politics. I left Sapucaia at an early age to go to Rio, and from there I went on to São Paulo for my degree. I returned only once to Sapucaia, to run for office, but I wasn't elected.

Actually, none of this information has anything to do with my adventure, but it is a way of saying something before actually entering into the heart of the matter, to which I find neither a large nor a small door. The best thing to do is to loosen my grip on my pen and let it go wandering about until it finds an entrance. There must be one—everything depends on the circumstances, a rule applicable as much to literary style as to life. Each word tugs another one along, one idea another, and that is how books, governments, and revolutions are made—some even say that is how Nature created her species.

Thus—back to the holy water and the door of the church. It was Saint Joseph's Church. Mass had ended. Claudina and Rosa made the sign of the cross on their foreheads, their thumbs moistened with holy water and gloveless only for this gesture. Then they adjusted their cloaks while I, in the doorway, surveyed the ladies who were leaving. Suddenly, I felt a pang of excitement, leaned out the doorway, and actually ended up taking two steps toward the street.

"What was it, cousin?"

"Nothing, nothing."

It was a lady who had passed right by the church, slowly, with bowed head, resting on her parasol as she strolled along; she was going up Misericórdia Street. To explain my excitement, it is necessary to say that this was the second time I had seen her. The first time had been at the Fluminense Racetrack, two months before, with a man who from all appearances was her husband, but who could just as easily have been her father. Her appearance was a bit ostentatious: she was dressed in scarlet with large, gaudy trimmings and wore a pair of earrings that were too heavy, but her eyes and mouth redeemed all the rest. The attraction was mutual, and we made no attempt to conceal it. If I say I fell for her, I won't be condemning my soul to hell, because it is the complete truth. I came away dumfounded, but I also came away disappointed, because I had lost sight of her in the crowd. I was unable to catch another glimpse of her, and no one was able to tell me who she might have been.

Imagine the displeasure I felt, knowing that fate had allowed her to cross my path again and that certain cousins of mine were standing in the way of my pursuing her. It shouldn't be difficult to imagine, because these cousins from Sapucaia come in all forms, and the reader is surely acquainted with them in one way or another. Sometimes they take the shape of a gentleman informed about the latest crisis in the ministry, who with a confidential air discloses to us all the events, both obvious and obscure, that led up to the crisis, as well as all old and new dissensions within the ministry and everything else pertaining to damaged interests, conspiracy, and catastrophe. At other times, these cousins disguise themselves as that eternal citizen who affirms in a ponderous and stuffy manner that there are no laws without traditions—that is, *nisi lege sine moribus*. Others don the mask of a street-corner Dangeau[1] and describe to us in great detail all the ribbons and lace trims that this, that, or the other lady wore to the ballet or to the theater. And during this time, the Opportunity passes by, slowly, with bowed head, resting on her parasol as she strolls along: she passes by, turns the corner, and good-by . . . Meanwhile, the ministry is seething with corruption, *nisi lege sine moribus*, the lady's dress is trimmed with malines and Brussels lace . . .

I was about to tell my cousins to go on ahead—we lived on Carmo Street, which wasn't far away—but I gave up the idea. Out in the street I also considered leaving them at church to wait for me, so that I might seize the Opportunity from behind. I even think I stopped for a moment, but I rejected this alternative as well and went on walking.

We continued walking away from the path of my mysterious lady. I glanced back many times until I lost sight of her in one of the turns in the street. She was staring at the ground as if contemplating something, day-dreaming, or waiting for a rendezvous. I'm not lying when I say this last idea made me jealous. I am exclusive and personal in my relationships, I would fare poorly as a lover of married women. It is unimportant that between myself and the lady there had existed only a few hours' dalliance from afar, because ever since I had become attracted to her, the barrier between us had become unbearable for me. I am also a dreamer—I soon invented an adventure and an adventurer and yielded to the morbid pleasure of suffering because of a purely imaginary situation. The cousins went on ahead of me, and they spoke to me from time to time. I barely answered them, if indeed I answered at all. In a cordial way I loathed them.

When we arrived at the door of the house, I consulted my watch as if I had something to do; then I told my cousins to go up and have lunch. I ran to Misericórdia Street. First I went to the School of Medicine, then I went back as far as the Chamber of Deputies, this time more slowly, expecting to see my lady as I arrived at each turn in the street, but there wasn't even a shadow of her. I was foolish, wasn't I? Just the same, I went up the street once more, because I realized that since she was traveling slowly and on foot, she would scarcely have had time to reach the middle of Santa Luzia Beach, if she had not stopped before then. Therefore, I continued my search up the street again and out to the beach, as far as the Ajuda Con-

---

1. Philippe, Marquis de Dangeau (1638–1720), an assiduous courtier who from 1684 to 1720 kept a journal, in which he meticulously recorded all the minute incidents that occurred at the court of Louis XIV.—Trans.

vent. I saw nothing, absolutely nothing. However, not even that discouraged me. I went back and retraced my steps at a pace which I thought would permit me to catch up with her. I even stopped and waited here and there in order not to miss her in case she had gone into a shop or someone's home. My entire body trembled as if I were actually going to see her at any moment. I understood the emotions of the insane.

Meanwhile, nothing. I went down the street without finding the least trace of my mysterious lady. Happy canines, who locate their friends through their sense of smell! Who knows if she weren't right there near by, inside a house, perhaps even her own house? I thought of inquiring, but of whom, and how? A baker, leaning against a portal, was watching me, and some women were doing the same thing, threading their eyes through the peepholes in their doors. They were of course wary of the passerby, the slow or hurried gait, the inquisitive glance, the nervous bearing. I let myself go on to the Chamber of Deputies and then stopped for five minutes, not knowing what to do next. It was almost noon. I waited for ten more minutes, then five more, standing up, hoping to see her. Finally, I gave up and went to lunch.

I didn't have lunch at home. I didn't want to see those devilish cousins who had stood in the way of my following the mysterious lady. I went to a hotel restaurant. I chose a table at the far end of the room and seated myself with my back to everyone else—I didn't wish to be seen or spoken to. I began to eat what they brought me. I asked for some newspapers, but I must confess that I didn't read continuously, and I scarcely understood three-fourths of what I was reading. In the middle of a news item or an article, my mind wandered off to Misericórdia Street, and I found myself at the door of the church, watching the anonymous lady pass by, slowly, with bowed head, resting on her parasol as she strolled along.

I managed to escape those two diabolical cousins of mine once more; on that occasion I was drinking my coffee and had a parliamentary speech in front of me. I found myself once again at the door of the church; I then imagined my cousins were not with me, and I was following the beautiful lady. This is how losers in the lottery console themselves; this is how frustrated ambitions are fulfilled.

Do not ask me to give details or explain the preliminaries of our meeting. Dreams disdain fine lines and finishing touches on landscapes—they content themselves with thick but representative brush strokes. My imagination leaped over the difficulties of the first conversation and went straight to Lavradio Street or Inválidos Street, to Adriana's very house. Her name was Adriana. She had not come to Misericórdia Street to rendezvous with anyone but merely to visit a relative or a friend, or perhaps a seamstress. We met and were equally thrilled. I wrote to her and she answered me. We pursued one another despite a multitude of moral codes and other dangers. Adriana was married; her husband was fifty-two, she about thirty. She had never loved anyone before, not even her husband, whom she had married out of obedience to her family. I taught her love and betrayal at the same time—this is what she told me in the cottage I rented outside the city especially for us.

Intoxicated, I listened to her. I wasn't mistaken about her, for she was indeed as ardent and loving as I had imagined her to be. I could read everything in her eyes—those bovine eyes of hers, large and round like Juno's. She lived for me alone. We wrote to each other every day, and despite this, each time we met in the cottage it was as if a century had gone by since our last meeting. I even thought her heart taught me something, in spite of its inexperience, or perhaps precisely because of it, for in matters of love one unlearns with practice, and the novice is the learned one. Adriana did not feign joy or tears—she wrote me what she thought and told me what she felt. She showed me that we were not two beings, but one, a universal being for whom God created the sun and the flowers, paper and ink, the postal service and closed carriages.

While I imagined all this, I believe I finished drinking my coffee. I recall that the waiter came to my table and removed the cup and the sugar bowl. I do not know if I asked him for a light—he probably saw me with the cigar in my hand and brought me the matches.

I won't swear to it, but I think I lit the cigar, because an instant later, through a veil of smoke, I saw my affectionate and beautiful Adriana resting on a sofa. I was on my knees, listening to her talk about her latest quarrel with her husband. He now distrusted her—she often left the house, became distracted or absorbed, or appeared sad or happy without reason, and he had begun to threaten her. Threaten her with what? I told her it would be better for her to leave him before he went too far and to come and openly live with me. Adriana listened to me pensively, like Eve, in love with the Devil, who murmured to her from without what her heart told her from within. Her fingers caressed my hair.

"Of course! Of course!"

She came the next day, alone, without a husband, without society, without scruples, completely alone, and from there we began to live together. No ostentation, no secrecy. We supposed ourselves foreigners, and we actually were nothing but that: we spoke a language no one had ever spoken or heard before. For centuries, all other love affairs had been veritable counterfeitings, for ours was the authentic edition. For the first time, the divine manuscript was being printed: it was a thick volume which we were dividing into as many chapters and paragraphs as there were days in a week or hours in a day. The design was woven of sun and music, the language was composed of the fine flowers of all other vocabularies. All gentle as well as vibrant words were extracted from them by the author to form this unique book—a book without an index, because it was infinite; without margins, so that Tedium could not write its notes in them; without a marker, because it was not necessary for us to interrupt our reading and mark the page.

A voice called me back to reality. It was a friend who had awakened late and had come to have lunch. This other cousin from Sapucaia would not even allow me to dream in peace! Five minutes later, I said good-by to him and left. I had been daydreaming for two hours.

It annoys me to have to admit that I returned to Misericórdia Street, but I must tell all: I went and found nothing. I returned on several other occasions and came home each time without any reward for all my wasted time and efforts. I resigned myself to foregoing the adventure or awaiting fate's solution. My cousins thought I was bored or ill, and I told them nothing to the contrary. Eight days later they went on their way without giving me cause to miss them—I bade them farewell as if they were a malign fever.

The image of my mysterious lady stayed with me for many weeks. In the street I was fooled many times. Sometimes I spotted a figure far away which looked exactly like her, and I trailed it closely until I caught up and saw I was mistaken. I began to think myself ridiculous, but every so often some remote shadow reminded me of Adriana, and the preoccupation was revived. Finally, other concerns arose and I ceased to think about her.

At the beginning of the following year, I went to Petrópolis. I made the trip with an old classmate, Oliveira, who had been a district attorney in Minas Gerais but had recently abandoned his career because of an inheritance he had received. He was as cheerful as he had been in our academy days, but from time to time he became silent and stared out of the boat or the carriage like someone who feebly attempts to revive his soul with remembrance, hope, or desire. At the mountaintop, I asked him which hotel he was going to. He responded that he was going to a private home, but did not tell me where, and evaded further discussion of the subject. I had expected him to visit me the next day, but he neither visited me nor did I see him anywhere. Another schoolmate of ours had heard he had a house somewhere near the Renânia district of Petrópolis.

None of these details would have come to mind had it not been for the news I received days later. Oliveira had run away with a married woman and taken refuge with her in Petrópolis. I was given both the woman's name and her husband's name. Hers was Adriana. I confess that although the name of my lady was entirely my own invention, I was startled to hear it—could they be one and the same woman? I saw right away that this was asking a great deal of Chance. This poor servant of human affairs already does enough by occasionally adjusting scattered threads. To require that he tie them all together again and reattach them to their original headings is to leap out of reality into romance. That was what common sense told me, but never did I utter an absurdity so seriously: the two women were indeed one and the same.

I saw her three weeks later when I went to visit Oliveira, who had arrived ill from Rio. We had gone up together the evening before. During our ascent he began to feel uncomfortable, and by the time we reached the summit he was feverish. I accompanied him to his house in the carriage, but I didn't enter because he didn't want me to go out of my way. The next day I went to see him, a bit out of friendship, another bit out of curiosity to meet the mysterious lady. I saw her . . . it was she, my one and only Adriana.

Oliveira recovered quickly but in spite of my enthusiasm in visiting him, he did not invite me to his house: he limited himself to seeing me at the hotel. I respected his motives, but at the same time they revived my old preoccupation. I considered the possibility that besides his concern for decorum, there might be jealousy on his part, brought on by his love for Adriana, and that either or both of these factors could be proof of a complex of refined and admirable qualities in the woman. That alone was enough to vex me, but the idea that her passion might be as great as his, along with the image of this couple comprising one body and soul, excited all the nerves of envy in me. I failed in all my efforts to set foot in his house and went so far as to tell him about the rumor that was circulating. He simply smiled and changed the subject.

The season in Petrópolis ended, but he stayed on. I believe he returned to Rio in July or August. At the end of the year, we happened to run into each other, and I found him somewhat taciturn and preoccupied. I saw him on other occasions, and he didn't seem to have changed, except that in addition to his taciturnity there was a definite air of unhappiness about him. I imagined that his suffering had been brought on by his love affair, and as I am not here to deceive anyone, I'll add that I experienced a feeling of pleasure. However, this feeling didn't last long—it was the work of the devil I carry within me, who usually turns these pleasures into a mountebank's grimaces. I punished him quickly and replaced him with an angel I also have, and I took pity on the poor boy, whatever the reason for his wretchedness might have been.

A neighbor of his, a friend of ours, told me something which confirmed my suspicions of domestic troubles, but it was he himself who told me everything one day, when I rashly asked him what had changed him so.

"What could it be? Imagine that I bought a lottery ticket and wasn't even fortunate enough to have won nothing at all. Instead, I drew a huge share of bad luck."

And as I perhaps frowned inquisitively, he added: "Ah! If you only knew half the things that have happened to me! Do you have time? Let's go to the Passeio Público."[2]

We entered the gardens and proceeded down one of the tree-lined paths. He told me everything, spending two hours counting the beads on an infinite rosary of miseries. The narration brought to light the incompatible temperaments of Oliveira and Adriana, united by sin or a perverse sort of love. They were sick of each other, yet condemned to intimacy and mutual aversion. He could neither leave nor tolerate her. No esteem, no respect, infrequent and imperfect happiness—a life completely ruined.

"Ruined," he repeated, nodding his head. "You don't have to see it, my life is completely ruined. You must remember our plans from the academy, when you aspired to be minister of the empire and I to be minister of justice. You can have both offices, I'll never be anything, ever. This egg, which should have hatched an eagle, will never even hatch a chicken. It's completely ruined. It's been this way for a year and a half, and I find no way out whatsoever. I've lost all sense of ambition . . ."

When I saw him six months later, he was miserable and distracted. Adriana had left him; she was pursuing geometry with a student from the Old Central School. "It's for the best," I told him. Oliveira stared at the ground, ashamed. He said good-by to me and went running off in search of her. He found her several weeks later—they left no word unsaid between them, and in the end they were reconciled. I then began to visit them with the intention of separating them. She was still beautiful and fascinating. Her manners were refined and tender but obviously hypocritical, accompanied by certain attitudes and gestures whose underlying intent was to entice me and carry me away.

I was afraid, and I retreated. She was not ashamed—she cast off her cloak of hypocrisy and was restored to her true self. I saw then that she was cold, scheming, unjust, often vulgar, and in certain situations I noticed a shade of perversity in her. At first, Oliveira laughed off all her accusations to make me believe she had lied or exaggerated: it was his shame of his

2. The Passeio Público (literally "public park") is located in southern Rio de Janeiro. Construction began in 1799 and was completed in 1803. Throughout the nineteenth century, the Passeio Público was one of the most popular recreational areas in Rio.—Trans.

own weakness. But he could not keep his mask on. She impiously tore it from him one day, revealing the humiliations he suffered when I was not present. I felt revulsion for the woman and pity for the miserable devil. I openly urged him to leave her. He hesitated, but promised to do it.

"Really, I can't take it any longer . . ."

We arranged everything, but at the last moment he could not bring himself to go through with the separation. She intoxicated him once more with her huge bovine eyes, the eyes of a basilisk, and this time—oh, my dear cousins from Sapucaia!—this time only to leave him exhausted and dead.

ALEXANDRIAN TALE

CHAPTER 1. AT SEA

"What, my dear Stroibus! No, impossible! No one will ever believe that the blood of a rat, given to a man to drink, could turn him into a thief."

"In the first place, Pythias, you are omitting one condition: the rat must meet its end beneath the surgeon's scalpel if we are to capture that fragile essence which is to bring about the desired result. Second, now that you are pointing out the example of the rat, I will have you know I have already experimented with my theory and have indeed managed to produce a thief!"

"A genuine thief?"

"He stole my cloak thirty days after the experiment, but he left me the greatest happiness in the world: the proof of my theory. What did I lose?—a scrap of rough cloth. What did the universe gain?—the immortal truth. Yes, my dear Pythias, that is the eternal truth. The constitutive elements of the thief are contained in the blood of the rat, those of the patient man in that of the ox, and those of the daring man in that of the eagle . . ."

"Those of the wise man in that of the owl," interrupted Pythias, smiling.

"No, the owl is only an emblem, but the blood of a spider, if somehow we could transfer it to a human, would give that man the rudiments of geometry and musical sensitivity. With a flock of storks, swallows, or cranes I will make a vagabond out of a homebody. The blood of the turtledove contains the principle of conjugal fidelity, that of the peacock holds the basic elements of infatuation . . . In short, the gods placed the essence of all human capabilities in the animals of the earth, water, and air. The animals are the letters of the alphabet, and man is the syntax. This is my new philosophy, this is what I will reveal in great Ptolemy's court."

Pythias shook his head and stared out to sea. The ship was bound for Alexandria with its precious cargo of two philosophers, who would carry the fruits of enlightened reason to that repository of knowledge. The two were old friends, both of them widowers in their fifties. Their specialty was metaphysics, but they were also acquainted with physics, chemistry, medicine, and music. One of them, Stroibus, had become an excellent anatomist, having read Herophilus' treatises many times. Cyprus was the native land of both men, but since it is true that no one can be a prophet in his own country, the Cyprians had never paid due respect to the two philosophers. On the contrary, they were detested—the street urchins went to the extreme of jeering at them. However, this was not the reason which had prompted them to leave their homeland. One day, when Pythias returned from a journey, he proposed that he and his colleague go to Alexandria, where the arts and sciences were held in high esteem. Stroibus agreed, and the two departed. Only now, after having set sail, did the author of the new doctrine reveal it to his companion, along with all his recent meditations and experiments.

"It's done," said Pythias, raising his head. "I can neither confirm nor deny anything. I will study your theory, and if I find it is sound, I will take it upon myself to develop it and divulge it to the world."

"Long live Helios!" exclaimed Stroibus. "I can depend on you as my disciple."

CHAPTER 2. EXPERIMENTS

The Alexandrian youths did not look upon the two learned men with the contempt of their Cyprian counterparts. Egypt was as solemn as the ibis perched on one leg, as pensive as a sphinx, as judicious as the mummies, as severe as the pyramids—there was neither time nor disposition for laughter. City and court, which had heard news of the two friends for some time, gave them a regal welcome, demonstrated a knowledge of their works, discussed their ideas, and showered them with gifts—papyri, crocodiles, zebras, purple robes. However, everything was humbly refused, with the explanation that a philosopher needed nothing more than philosophy and that the superfluous would only act as a deterrent to their scientific pursuits. Such a noble reply filled all Alexandrians, from the wise men and the leaders to the common people, with admiration. The most sagacious commented: "What else could be expected of two such distinguished men, who in their magnificent treatises . . ."

"We have in our possession something even greater than those treatises," interrupted Stroibus. "I have brought a theory which will soon govern the universe, for I intend to do no less than reconstitute men and nations by redistributing talents and virtues."

"But shouldn't that be the gods' work?" someone objected.

"I have uncovered the gods' secret," ventured Stroibus. "Mankind is the syntax of nature, and I have discovered the laws of divine grammar . . ."

"Explain yourself."

"Later. Let me experiment first. When my doctrine is complete, I will reveal it as the greatest gift mankind could ever receive from a single man."

One can imagine the public's expectations and the other philosophers' curiosity, even though everyone was reluctant to believe that the new truth could eventually replace those they had always possessed. Nevertheless, everyone waited anxiously. The two visitors were pointed out on the streets even by small children. A son dreamed of transforming his father's greed, a father his son's foolishness, a lady a certain gentleman's indifference, a gentleman a certain lady's whims, because all Egypt, from the Pharaohs to the Ptolemies, was the land of Potiphar, Potiphar's wife, Joseph's many-colored coat, and all the rest. Stroibus became the great hope of the city and the world.

After studying the doctrine, Pythias confronted Stroibus and warned him: "Metaphysically speaking, your theory is preposterous, but I am willing to allow you one experiment, provided that it be decisive. There is only one way, my dear Stroibus, in which this experiment can be carried out. Due to our cultivation of reason as much as our steadfastness of character, you and I constitute the strongest possible opposition to the vice of thievery. Therefore, if you manage to successfully implant this vice in us, nothing further will be necessary. If you fail to bring about this result (which is more than likely, since the entire idea is utterly absurd), you will abandon all thoughts of such a theory and return to our former meditations."

Stroibus accepted the proposal. "My sacrifice will be the most painful one," he said, "as I am certain of the outcome of it all, but is there anything that Truth does not deserve? Truth is immortal, man is but a brief moment . . ."

If the Egyptian rats had known about Stroibus' plan, they would have imitated the early Hebrews, who chose to flee toward the desert rather than accept the new doctrine. And we can believe that such a flight would have resulted in disaster. Science, like war, has its imperious necessities, and since the rats' ignorance and weakness, along with the mental and physical superiority of the two philosophers, were such great advantages in favor of the experiment, it was fitting to seize this magnificent opportunity to learn if, in effect, the source of human passions and virtues was to be found among the animal species and whether it was possible to transmit it to humans.

Stroibus caged the rats and subjected them to the knife one by one. After winding strips of cloth around each victim's snout and feet, he tied the animal's neck and legs to the dissecting table. When this was done, he made the first incision in the chest, very slowly, gradually inserting the scalpel until it touched the heart, for it was his opinion that instantaneous death would contaminate the blood, destroy the sought-after essence, and thus render it useless for experimental purposes. An able anatomist, he operated with a resoluteness that befitted his scientific objective. A less skillful surgeon would have frequently interrupted the procedure because the victims' spasms of pain and agony made the handling of the scalpel awkward. But this was precisely Stroibus' superiority: he possessed the trained, unflinching self-assuredness of a master surgeon.

At Stroibus' side, Pythias collected the blood and assisted with the operations, restraining the patients' convulsive movements and observing the progress of the agony in the animals' eyes. The observations made by each scientist were recorded separately on sheets of papyrus, and in this manner science benefited in two ways. At times, due to differing observations, they were obliged to dissect a greater number of rats than was necessary, but even so there was no waste involved, since the blood of the additional rats was set aside to be ingested later. Just one such incident will adequately illustrate the conscientiousness with which they carried out their work. Pythias had noted that the retinas of the dying rats changed in color until they became a light blue, while Stroibus' observations indicated a cinnamon color as the final shade at death. They had reached the last dissection of the day, but as the point was well worth investigating, despite their fatigue they experimented nineteen more times without obtaining conclusive results—Pythias continued to insist on blue, Stroibus on the cinnamon color. The twentieth rat almost brought about agreement between them, but with great sagacity Stroibus realized that his stance had changed. He corrected it, and they dissected twenty-five more rats. Of these, the first one still left them in doubt, but the remaining twenty-four proved that the disputed color was neither cinnamon nor blue, but a pale shade of violet.

Exaggerated accounts of the experiments caused a great stir within the sentimental element of the city and stimulated the garrulity of certain sophists, but the earnest Stroibus (gently, so as not to injure even the most delicate realms of the human soul) responded that Truth was worth all the rats in the universe, not only all the rats, but all the peacocks, goats, dogs, nightingales, and so forth. In relation to the rats, the city as well as science would profit, because the curse of such a destructive animal would be diminished. Moreover, even if the same consideration were not applicable to other animals—such as turtledoves and dogs, which would be dissected in due time—the rights of Truth were no less inalienable. Nature should not only be the dinner table, he concluded aphoristically, but Science's table as well.

And they continued to extract and drink the blood. They did not drink it in a pure form but diluted it in a concoction of cinnamon, acacia sap, and balsam, which completely disguised its primitive flavor. The doses were daily and diminutive, and therefore it was necessary for them to wait a long time before the desired effect would be produced. Pythias, impatient and incredulous, scoffed at his colleague.

"Still nothing?"

"Be patient," Stroibus would tell him, "be patient. One does not acquire a vice in the same way one sews a pair of sandals."

CHAPTER 3. VICTORY

At last, Stroibus triumphed! The experiment proved his theory. Pythias was the first to exhibit the long-awaited symptoms, attributing to himself three ideas he had heard from Stroibus. Stroibus, in retaliation, stole four comparisons from Pythias, as well as a theory of the winds. What could be more scientific than these debut performances? The ideas of others, precisely because they cannot be bought on the street corner, have a certain public air about them, and it is very natural to begin with them before continuing on to borrowed books, hens, forged papers, entire provinces, and so on. The designation of plagiarism in itself is an indication that men understand the tendency to confuse that mere embryo of thievery with thievery proper.

It is painful to relate, but the truth is that both Stroibus and Pythias cast all their metaphysical baggage into the Nile and became full-fledged thieves. They always readied themselves in the evening and on the following day went for such items as cloaks, bronze pieces, amphoras of wine, merchandise from the docks, and sound drachmas. They were so discreet about their thievery that no one so much as suspected them, but even if someone had, how could he possibly have made anyone else believe him? By then Ptolemy had collected many treasures and rarities for his library, and since it was perhaps advisable that they be cataloged, he assigned five grammarians and five philosophers to the job, among them our two comrades. They worked at their task with singular dedication, being the first to arrive and the last to leave, often working by lamplight into the wee hours of the morning, deciphering, arranging, and classifying. The enthusiastic Ptolemy foresaw brilliant futures for both of them.

After some time, the absence of various important articles began to be noticed: a copy of Homer's works, three Persian and two Samaritan scrolls, a superb collection of Alexander's original letters, copies of Athenian laws, the second and third books of Plato's *Republic*, among others. The authorities were alerted, but the rat's shrewdness, transferred to a superior organism, was naturally all the more acute, and the two illustrious thieves simply mocked the spies and guards. They eventually established the philosophical precept of never leaving empty-handed: they invariably succeeded in pilfering some article, a fable if nothing else. Finally, as there was a ship ready to depart for Cyprus, they took their leave of Ptolemy with a promise to return, sewed the stolen books inside hippopotamus skins, attached false tags to them, and attempted to flee. But the other philosophers' jealousy could no longer be contained: the suspicious magistrates were prodded further, and the scandal was uncovered. Stroibus and Pythias were taken for adventurers who had disguised themselves under the names of those two distinguished gentlemen, and Ptolemy himself deposited them into the hands of the authorities with the firm order that they be executed immediately. It was then that Herophilus, father of the science of anatomy, intervened.

CHAPTER 4. PLUS ULTRA!

"Sire," he said to Ptolemy, "until now I have limited myself to the dissection of human cadavers. But a cadaver gives me only structure, not life—it provides me only the organs, not their functions. I need life and its functions."

"What are you saying?" bellowed Ptolemy. "Do you want to disembowel Stroibus' rats?"

"No, sire, I do not wish to disembowel rats."

"Dogs? Geese? Hares?"

"Nothing of the sort. I am asking for some live human subjects."

"Live human subjects? Impossible, out of the question . . ."

"I will show you that it is not only possible, but even legal and necessary. The prisons of Egypt are overflowing with criminals, who no doubt occupy the lowest position on the human scale. They are no longer citizens, nor can they even call themselves men, because they have lost the two principal human characteristics—reason and virtue—by violating law and morality. And besides, since they must atone for their crimes through death, would it not be fair to have them serve Truth and Science in the process? Truth is immortal. It is worth not only all the rats but all the criminals in the world as well."

Ptolemy found this reasoning flawless and commanded that all criminals be turned over to Herophilus and his followers. The great anatomist expressed his gratitude for such an extraordinary favor, and he began to dissect the condemned. The masses reacted with extreme consternation. However, with the exception of a few verbal petitions, there were no insurrections against the measure. Herophilus repeated the explanation he had given Ptolemy, adding that the subjection of the criminals to anatomical experiments was an indirect way of promoting morality, since the terror of the scalpel in itself would act as a deterrent to many crimes.

Upon leaving prison, none of the condemned suspected the scientific fate which awaited them. The prisoners were released one by one, occasionally by twos or threes. Many of them, stretched out and strapped on the operating table, never entertained a single doubt as to their fate: they imagined it was all a new method of speedy execution. Only when the anatomists disclosed the day's object of study, raised their scalpels, and made the first incisions did the unfortunate victims become aware of their true predicament. Those who could recall witnessing the experiments with the rats suffered doubly, because their imaginations brought together the suffering of the present and the spectacle of the past.

To conciliate Science's interests with Compassion's impulses, the prisoners were dissected successively rather than in view of one another. When they arrived by twos or threes, those waiting their turn were not placed in an area from which they could hear the screams from the operating room. Although their cries were often muffled by means of certain devices, they were never totally suppressed, and in certain cases the very object of the experiment required that the emission of the voice be unhindered. At times the operations were carried out simultaneously, but then they were performed in locations distant from each other.

Nearly fifty prisoners had been dissected when the day of Stroibus' and Pythias' execution arrived. When at last it was time for them to be taken away, they still assumed they would be sentenced to a judiciary death and accordingly entrusted their souls to the gods. On the way to their execution, they pilfered a few figs and explained the incident by attributing it to an impulse of hunger. Later on, however, they stole a flute, and they were unable to satisfactorily explain this action. Still, a thief's cunning is infinite, and Stroibus, in order to justify his recent action, attempted to play a few notes on the instrument. The Alexandrians were filled with compassion and pity, for all were well aware of the fate that would befall the two thieves. Herophilus astonished all his disciples with the announcement of the latest petty crimes.

"Seriously," said the master surgeon, "it is an extraordinary case, a beautiful case. But before we consider our main goal, let us first examine the other point . . ."

Their objective was to determine whether the principal nerve of thievery was found in the palm of the hand or in the tips of the fingers—this problem had been suggested by one of the students. Stroibus was the first to be subjected to the operation. He understood it all before entering the operating room, and as human nature does have a vilest part, he humbly asked that they spare the life of a philosopher. But Herophilus, the great dialectician, replied in the following manner: "You are either an adventurer or the real Stroibus. In the first case, you have here the sole means of redeeming yourself for the crime of deceiving an enlightened ruler—go now and lend yourself to the scalpel. In the second case, you must be aware that the obligation of a philosopher is to serve philosophy and that the body is worthless in comparison with knowledge."

This said, the experiment began with Stroibus' hands, which produced optimal results that were recorded in notebooks, later lost with the decline of the Ptolemies. Pythias' hands were also dissected and meticulously examined. The pathetic victims screamed, wept, and pleaded, but Herophilus calmly reminded them that the duty of the philosopher was to serve philosophy and that in relation to the goals of science, they were even more valuable than rats, since it was obviously much more valid to draw conclusions about humans from men than from rats. He continued to dissect them, fiber by fiber, for eight days. On the third day, their eyes were extracted to virtually disprove a certain theory regarding the eye's inner structure. The removal of both men's stomachs is not worth discussing, as it involved a problem of secondary importance which, in any case, had been studied and resolved in five or six individuals dissected previously.

The Alexandrians reported that the rats commemorated this distressing and lamentable incident with dances and feasts, to which they invited a number of dogs, turtledoves, peacocks, and other animals which had been threatened with the same fate. It was also rumored that none of the invitations was accepted, at the suggestion of a certain dog which melancholically observed: "There will come a time when the same thing could happen to us." To which one of the rats was said to have replied: "But until then, let us laugh!"

THE DEVIL'S CHURCH

CHAPTER 1. A MARVELOUS IDEA

An old Benedictine manuscript relates that one day the Devil took it into his head to found a church. Though his profits were continuous and sizable, he was humiliated by the odd role he had played for centuries, which lacked organization, rules, canons, rituals. He lived, so to speak, off divine leftovers, human favors, and oversights. Nothing definite, nothing regular. Why shouldn't he have his own church? A Devil's Church would be the effective means to combat the other religions and destroy them once and for all.

"Well, then, a church," he concluded. "Scripture against scripture, breviary against breviary. I'll have my own mass, with wine and bread galore, my own sermons, bulls, novenas, and all the other religious trappings. My creed will be the universal nucleus of spirits, my church one of Abraham's tents. And then while the other religions quarrel and split, my church will be unique. Neither Mohammed nor Luther will surpass me. There are many ways to affirm, there is only one way to deny everything."

As he said this, the Devil shook his head and held out his arms in a magnificent virile gesture. He immediately reminded himself to go to God, confront Him with his idea, and challenge Him. The Devil then lifted his eyes, aflame with hate, harsh with vengeance, and said to himself: "Let's go, it's time." And quickly, beating his wings together with a commotion that shook all the provinces of the abyss, he ascended from the shadows into the infinite blue.

CHAPTER 2. BETWEEN GOD AND THE DEVIL

God was receiving an old man when the Devil arrived in Heaven. The seraphs bedecking the new arrival with garlands stopped their work immediately, and the Devil remained at the entrance with his eyes on the Lord.

"What do you want of Me?" asked the Lord.

"I haven't come on behalf of Your servant Faust," answered the Devil with a snicker, "but on behalf of all Fausts of all centuries."

"Explain yourself."

"Lord, the explanation is simple, but first allow me to say this to You: take in this good old gentleman, give him the best place in Heaven, order the most divinely tuned zithers and lutes to receive him with the most divine choruses . . ."

"Do you know what he did?" asked the Lord, His eyes full of tenderness.

"No, but he'll probably be one of the last ones to come to You. It won't be long before Heaven will be like a hotel that is empty because of its high rates. I'm going to build a cheap boardinghouse, that is, I'm going to found my own church. I'm tired of my disorganization and my haphazard, adventitious reign. It's time for me to win a final and complete victory. I came to tell You this out of loyalty, so You won't accuse me of being underhanded. Good idea, don't You think?"

"You came to tell Me about it, not to legitimize it," the Lord pointed out.

"You're right," answered the Devil, "but vanity enjoys hearing applause from the masters. It's true that in this case it will be the applause of a defeated master, and . . . Lord, I'm going to descend to Earth and lay down my cornerstone."

"Go ahead."

"Do You want me to come back and report on how everything turns out?"

"That won't be necessary. Just tell Me why, after being dissatisfied with your disorganization for so long, did it only now occur to you to found your own church?"

The Devil smiled with an air of mockery and triumph. He had a cruel idea in his soul, a searing comment in the saddlebag of his memory, something that made him believe he was superior to God Himself in that brief instant of eternity. However, he held back his laughter and said:

"Only now have I finished an observation I began several centuries ago—I have seen that virtues, daughters of Heaven, are to a great extent comparable to queens whose velvet cloaks are trimmed with cotton fringes. Now I propose to pull them by those fringes and bring them all to my church. Behind them will come the fringes of pure silk . . ."

"Stale rhetoric!" muttered the Lord.

"But look. Many such bodies who kneel at Your feet in the temples of the world come in bustles from the drawing room and the street, their faces tinted with the same powder, their kerchiefs all smelling the same, and their eyes sparkling with curiosity and devotion between the holy book and the mustache of sin. Look at the eagerness—the indifference, at least—with which that gentleman publicizes the benefits he liberally distributes—clothes, boots, coins, or any other materials necessary to life . . . But I don't want it to seem that I'm picking on insignificant details. For example, I'm not talking about the self-satisfaction with which that lay brother piously wears Your love and a religious medal at his breast in the processions . . . I'm talking about more important things . . ."

With this the seraphs flapped their wings, which were heavy with boredom and fatigue. Michael and Gabriel eyed the Lord imploringly. God interrupted the Devil:

"You are banal, which is the worst thing that could happen to a spirit of your kind. Everything you're saying or may say has already been said and resaid by the moralists of the world. It's a hackneyed subject, and if you haven't enough resourcefulness or originality to restate it in a new light, it would be best for you to be quiet and forget about it. Look, the faces of all My legions show marked signs of the boredom you're causing them. That old man looks nauseated, and do you know what he did?"

"I already told You I don't know."

"After living an honest life, he died a sublime death. Caught in a shipwreck, he was going to save himself by clinging to a plank, but he saw two newlyweds, in the flower of youth, who were already grappling with death. He gave them the life-saving plank and dove off into eternity. No one witnessed this deed, for he was surrounded only by water and the sky above it. Where do you see the cotton fringe in that?"

"Lord, as You know, I am the spirit who denies."

"Do you deny the selflessness of this death?"

"I deny everything. Misanthropy can take on the appearance of charity—for a misanthrope, leaving life to others is the same as showing hatred for them . . ."

"Sly and rhetorical!" exclaimed the Lord. "Go, go ahead and found your church, call on all the virtues, gather all the fringes, convoke all men . . . But go, get out of here!"

In vain the Devil attempted to call out something else. God imposed silence upon him. At a divine signal, the seraphs filled the heavens with the harmonies of their canticles. The Devil suddenly felt himself airborne—he folded his wings and fell to Earth like a bolt of lightning.

CHAPTER 3. GOOD NEWS FOR MANKIND

Once on Earth, the Devil did not waste a minute. He hurriedly slipped on a Benedictine robe, since it was a habit of good reputation, and began to broadcast a new and extraordinary doctrine with a voice that echoed throughout the depths of the century. He promised his disciples and the faithful all the earthly delights, all the glories and most intimate pleasures. He confessed he was the Devil, but he confessed it in order to rectify men's notions about him and to disavow the tales pious old women told about him.

"Yes, I am the Devil," he repeated, "not the Devil of sulfurous nights and soporific tales, or the terror of children, but the one and only true Devil, the genius of nature who was given that name in order to remove him from the hearts of men. See how well-bred and pleasant I am. I am your true father. Come, follow me and embrace that name which was invented for my dishonor, make an emblem and a standard out of it, and I'll give you everything, everything . . ."

He spoke in this manner in order to excite enthusiasm and enliven the indifferent, in other words, to congregate the multitudes around him. And they came. As soon as they arrived, the Devil proceeded to define his doctrine. In regard to its substance, it was what one could expect from the spirit who denies—as for its form, it was sometimes very refined and at other times impudent and shameless.

He proclaimed that the accepted virtues ought to be replaced by others which were the natural, legitimate ones. Vanity, lust, and sloth were reinstated, as was avarice, which he declared was only the mother of economy, the difference between the two being that the mother was robust and the daughter skin and bones. Anger had its best justification in the existence of Homer—without Achilles' fury there would have been no *Iliad*: "Muse, sing the wrath of Achilles, son of Peleus . . ." He said the same about gluttony, which produced Rabelais' finest pages and many good verses in Cruz e Silva's *Hissope*.[1] It was such a superior virtue that no one remembers Lucullus' battles, only his banquets: it was gluttony that really immortalized him. But even if one were to disregard these literary and historical arguments and consider only the intrinsic value of gluttony, who would deny that it was much better to feel an abundance of good food in the mouth and belly than meager mouthfuls or the saliva of fasting? The Devil promised to replace the Lord's vineyard, a metaphorical expression, with the Devil's vineyard, a straightforward and real locution, since he would never fail to provide his flock with the fruit of the world's most beautiful vines. As for envy, he preached coldly that it was the principal virtue, the origin of infinite prosperities, a delightful sentiment which supplemented all other virtues and talents.

The crowds ran after him enthusiastically. With great gusts of eloquence, the Devil instilled the new order of things in his followers, changing their notions about the world, making them love the perverse and detest the wholesome.

For example, there was nothing more curious than his definition of dishonesty. He called it man's left arm, the right arm being strength, and his conclusion was simply that many men are left-handed. He did not require that all men be left-handed—he wasn't an exclusivist. He accepted those who were either right- or left-handed but not those who were neither. His most profound, rigorous explanation was that of venality: one casuist of the time even confessed that it was a monument of logic. Venality, said the Devil, was the exercise of a right superior to all others. If you can sell your house, ox, shoe, or hat—things that legally and juridically belong to you—why is it that you cannot sell your opinion, vow, word, or faith—things more valuable than mere possessions because they are elements of your conscience, that is, your very self? To deny this would be to fall into absurdity and contradiction. Don't some women sell their hair? Can't a man sell some of his blood to transfuse it into another, anemic man? Are blood and hair—parts of the body—more privileged than character—the moral part of a man? Thus having demonstrated the principle of venality, the Devil did not delay in expounding its worldly and pecuniary benefits. Then, he showed that in view of social prejudice, it would be appropriate to disguise the execution of such a legitimate right. In doing so, one would

1. *O Hissope*, literally *The Aspergillum*, a satirical poem by the Portuguese poet Antônio Dinis da Cruz e Silva (1731–1799).—Trans.

exercise venality and hypocrisy at the same time and would thus become doubly worthy.

He was everywhere at the same time, examining and rectifying everything. He naturally combated forgiveness for wrongs and other principles of kindness and cordiality. Though he did not categorically prohibit slander without payment, he encouraged that it always be practiced with some form of remuneration in mind, monetary or otherwise. However, when slander was solely an uncontrollable expansion of the imagination, he prohibited the receipt of any salary, for this was equivalent to being paid for breathing. He condemned the use of all forms of respect, citing them as possible elements of social and personal decorum, except when an obsequious display of respect was necessary for achieving personal gain. However, this exception was eventually eliminated by the fact that the desire for personal gain converted respect into mere flattery—hence flattery, not respect, was actually the applied sentiment in such cases.

To finish off his work, the Devil believed it would be appropriate to destroy all human solidarity, seeing that the concept of love for one's fellow man was a serious obstacle to his new institution. He showed that this concept was the simple invention of parasites and insolvent businessmen, for one should show nothing but indifference—and in some cases, hate or contempt—toward one's fellow man. He went so far as to demonstrate that the notion of one's "fellow man" was erroneous by quoting these lines from the cultured and refined Neapolitan priest, Fernando Galiani, who wrote to one of the Marchionesses of the old regime: "To hell with fellow men! There are no fellow men!" The only situation in which the Devil allowed someone to love his fellow man was that of loving another man's wife, because this kind of love had the peculiarity of being nothing more than the individual's love for himself. And as some disciples may have found that such a metaphysical explanation escaped the comprehension of the masses, the Devil had recourse to an apologue: one hundred people take out shares of stock in a bank, for common operations, but each shareholder is only concerned with his own dividends. That is what happens with adulterers. This fable was included in the Devil's book of wisdom.

CHAPTER 4. FRINGES AND MORE FRINGES

The Devil's prophecy came true. All the virtues whose velvet cloaks ended in cotton fringes left their cloaks in the nettles and came to join the new church after their fringes had been tugged. Others followed them, and time blessed the institution. The church had been founded; the doctrine was being spread; there was not one region of the globe that was not acquainted with it, one language into which it had not been translated, or one race that did not love it. The Devil raised shouts of triumph.

However, one day, many years later, the Devil noticed that many of the faithful secretly practiced the old virtues. They did not practice all of them, nor did they practice them completely, but they did practice some of them partially and as has already been said, secretly. Certain gluttons retreated three or four times per year to eat frugally, precisely on days designated by Catholic regime. Many misers gave alms at night or on sparsely populated streets. Various defrauders of the treasury occasionally returned small quantities to it. At one time or another, dishonest men told the unadulterated truth, but they maintained the usual deceitful expressions on their faces in order to give the impression of fraudulence.

This discovery alarmed the Devil. He began to observe the evil more closely and saw that it was greatly increasing. Some cases were incomprehensible, like that of a Levantine druggist who had long been poisoning an entire generation of a certain family but who rescued the victims' children with the by-products of the drugs. In Cairo, the Devil found an unrepentant camel thief who covered his face so he could go into the mosques. The Devil confronted him at the entrance to a mosque and directly reproached him for his behavior, but the thief denied the accusations, saying he was going to the mosque to steal a camel from a dragoman. However, after stealing it in the Devil's presence, he gave it as a gift to a muezzin who prayed to Allah for him. The Benedictine manuscript cites many other extraordinary discoveries, among them the following one, which completely disoriented the Devil. One of his best disciples was a Calabrian, fifty years of age, a celebrated forger of documents who had a beautiful house in the Roman countryside, with paintings, statues, and a library. He was deceit in person—he even took to his bed in order to avoid confessing he was healthy. However, the Devil discovered that not only did this man not cheat at gambling, he even gave gratuities to his servants. After winning the friendship of a clergyman, he went to him every week to confess himself in a solitary chapel, and although he did not reveal any of his secret activities to his friend, he always crossed himself twice, once when he kneeled and again when he stood up. The Devil could hardly believe such treachery, but there was no doubt about it—the case was real.

He did not waste an instant. The shock gave him no time to reflect, compare, or conclude from the present spectacle anything analogous with the past. He soared up to Heaven again, trembling with rage, anxious to find out the secret cause of such a singular phenomenon. God listened to him with infinite satisfaction but did not interrupt or answer him nor did He even gloat over that satanic agony. He looked the Devil straight in the eye and said:

"What did you expect, My poor Devil? The cotton cloaks now have silken fringes, just as those of velvet had cotton fringes. What did you expect? It's the eternal human contradiction."

A STRANGE THING

"The strangest things happen. Do you see that lady who's headed toward the Church of the Holy Cross? She just stopped in the churchyard to give alms."

"The woman dressed in black?"

"Precisely. There, she's entering now."

"Say no more. The look on your face tells me she's an old flame, and not so old at that, judging from her figure. She's really a beauty."

"She's about forty-six now."

"Ah, and well preserved! Come on, stop staring at the ground and tell me everything. Is she a widow?"

"No."

"Then her husband's still living. Is he old?"

"She's not married."

"Single?"

"In a manner of speaking. I think she's called Dona Maria now. In 1860 she was known by the familiar name of Marocas. She wasn't a seamstress, shopkeeper, or schoolmistress—just keep eliminating the professions and you'll get there. When she lived on Sacramento Street she was narrow-waisted and, of course, prettier than she is now. Her behavior and speech were refined and beyond reproach. Although she dressed most properly and unostentatiously, many men fell for her."

"You, for example?"

"No. But Andrade, a friend of mine from Alagoas, went for her. At the time he was twenty-six, half lawyer and half politician. He was married in Bahia and came here in 1859. His wife was beautiful, gracious, gentle, and resigned. When I met them they had a little two-year-old daughter."

"You mean to tell me he had all that, and Marocas was still able to . . . ?"

"That's right, she bewitched him. Look, if you're not in a hurry, I'll tell you an interesting story."

"Please do."

"He was near the entrance of Paula Brito's bookstore in the Rocio when he first met her. He saw a lovely woman coming in his direction. He awaited her with excited anticipation, because he was an inveterate skirt-chaser. As Marocas approached him she stopped, looking as though she were searching for an address. She stopped again in front of Brito's store. Then, with embarrassment and apprehension, she handed Andrade a piece of paper and asked him how she could get to the address written on it. He told her it was on the other side of the Rocio and pointed to the probable location. She curtsied gracefully and left. But Andrade was at a loss to explain the meaning of that encounter."

"So am I."

"It's simple. Although Andrade could never have guessed it at the time, Marocas didn't know how to read. At any rate, he watched her cross the Rocio, which then had no statue or garden. She kept inquiring at other doors until she found the place she was looking for. That same evening, Andrade went to the Ginásio Theater, where *Camille* was playing. Marocas was there and wept like a child during the last act. Need I say more? Within two weeks they were madly in love. Marocas dismissed all her suitors—and the loss was considerable, because several of them were wealthy entrepreneurs. She lived completely alone with no interest in life other than Andrade, on whom she lavished all her attentions."

"Just like Camille?"

"Exactly. Andrade taught her to read. 'I've become a schoolteacher,' he said. And that's how he came to tell me about their first meeting in the Rocio. Marocas learned quickly, which is understandable: she was probably embarrassed by her lack of knowledge and wanted to understand the novels he talked about. In brief, she wanted to please him and live up to his expectations. Andrade concealed nothing from me, and you can't imagine how his eyes shone when he mentioned her name. I was also Marocas' confidant.

"The three of us used to dine together, and—I see no reason to deny it—sometimes his wife would join us. Don't think for a moment that our dinners were unseemly affairs—they were lively, but dignified and proper. In matters of language as well as dress, Marocas was refined. After a time our relationship became close, and she showered me with questions about Andrade's life. What were his tastes? Did he really care for her, or was she just a passing fancy? Were there other women in his life, and would he easily forget her? This torrent of questions and her fear at the thought of losing him revealed the depth and sincerity of her affection. On Saint John's Day, Andrade took his family to the festival in Gávea. I accompanied them, and we were gone for two days. When we said good-by to Marocas, she told us that our departure made her think about the play *I'll Dine with Mother*, which she had seen a few weeks before at the Ginásio Theater. Since she had no family to join on Saint John's Day, she said she would dine with a portrait as Sophie Arnould had done in the play, but it would be Andrade's portrait because she didn't have a mother. This display of devotion moved Andrade, and he leaned over to kiss her, but she saw me standing there and discreetly held him back with her hands."

"I like that gesture."

"So did Andrade. He gently cupped her face in his hands and gave her a paternal kiss on the forehead. Then we departed for Gávea. On our way, Andrade said the most flattering things about Marocas. He went into great detail, even about the inconsequential things they had most recently discussed or done together. He also mentioned that he planned to buy her a house in the suburbs as soon as he had the money. In passing, he praised her thriftiness, saying that she would accept only the bare essentials from him. To illustrate his point, I related an incident he didn't know about: three weeks before, Marocas had pawned some jewels to pay her seamstress. This news moved him deeply. I can't swear to it, but I think there were tears in his eyes. At any rate, he told me that after further consideration he had definitely decided to buy her a house in order to spare her any more hardship. In Gávea, we continued to talk about Marocas until the end of the holiday. When we returned, Andrade dropped his family off at their home in the Lapa district, then went to his office to dispatch some papers that required immediate attention. Shortly after noon, a man named Leandro appeared in Andrade's office and asked him for the usual five to ten dollars. Leandro, a former scribe of a lawyer friend of Andrade's, was a good-for-nothing rascal who made a habit of imposing on his exemployer's friends. Andrade gave him a ten-dollar bill and seeing that he was all smiles, asked him if he'd swallowed a canary. Leandro winked and moistened his lips. Andrade, who relished erotic stories, asked Leandro if he were having an affair. After a moment's hesitation, he confessed that he was."

"Look . . . isn't that Marocas coming out of the church now?"

"It certainly is—let's move away from the corner."

"Really, she must have been an extremely beautiful woman. She has a kind of regal quality about her."

"She didn't look in our direction, she never looks to the side. Now she's going up Ouvidor Street."

"Yes, I'm beginning to understand Andrade."

"I'll get to the point. Leandro confessed that the evening before he had had a rare, if not unique, stroke of luck that he had neither expected nor deserved, because he knew he was just a poor devil. But the poor are also children of God. It so happened that the night before in the Rocio, at about ten o'clock, he had come across a simply dressed, attractive woman completely enveloped in a large shawl. The lady approached him from behind, walking briskly and looking at him with unusual persistence as she brushed past him, and she walked on as though she expected him to make a move. The poor devil imagined that she had mistaken him for someone else and confessed to Andrade that despite her simple clothing, he saw at once she was out of his class. He kept on walking and the woman, who had stopped, once again fixed her eyes on him, this time with such insistence that he summoned up the courage to make a pass at her—she did the rest for him. Ah, what an angel! And she had a first-rate house with a classy living room! It was enough to make a man's mouth water, and all for free. 'Look,' he told Andrade, 'this would be the perfect set-up for you!' Andrade shook his head and told Leandro he wasn't interested in adulterous affairs. But Leandro insisted, saying that she lived on Sacramento Street, number . . ."

"You can't mean it!"

"You can imagine Andrade's reaction. For a while he didn't know what to do, say, think, or feel. When he regained enough composure to ask Leandro if he were telling the truth, Leandro called his attention to the fact that he had no reason to invent such a story. But when he saw Andrade's concern over the matter, he asked him to keep it a secret and said that he, for his part, would be discreet. When Leandro got up to leave, Andrade stopped him and asked, 'Do you want to make some money?' 'Sure, what do you want me to do?' 'I'll give you fifty dollars if you'll go to the lady's house with me and tell me in her presence that she's the one you were with.'"

"That's terrible!"

"I'm not defending Andrade—it was really an ugly situation. But in such cases, love blinds the best of men. Andrade was honorable, generous, and sincere, but the wound was so deep and he loved her so much that he was unable to refrain from striking back at her."

"Did Leandro accept the proposition?"

"Not right away. I think he hesitated momentarily out of fear, rather than a sense of propriety. But fifty dollars was a lot of money, so he accepted on the condition that Andrade not get him into trouble because of it. When Andrade entered Marocas' house, she was in the living room. She went to embrace him, but Andrade let her know he had brought someone else with him. Then, looking at her very closely, he asked Leandro to enter. Marocas grew pale. 'Is this the same lady?' he asked. 'Yes, sir,' mumbled Leandro in a faint voice—because some actions are even baser than the people who commit them. With great affectation, Andrade opened his wallet, took out a fifty-dollar bill, handed it to Leandro, and asked him to leave. The scene that followed his departure was brief but dramatic. I didn't get the complete story because Andrade was obviously so stunned by the incident that many of the details escaped him. Although Marocas confessed nothing, she was clearly beside herself. When Andrade dashed for the door, after venting his anger, she threw herself at his feet in desperation, weeping and threatening to take her life. She was lying prostrate on the floor at the top of the staircase when Andrade descended the stairs and departed in a rush."

"Do you mean she actually went out into the streets and picked up an absolute good-for-nothing? She must have made a habit of that sort of thing."

"No."

"She didn't?"

"Let me finish. It was probably eight o'clock that evening when Andrade went to my house and waited for me. He had already been there three times looking for me. I was astonished when he told me what had happened, but how could I doubt someone who had taken the precaution to prove his case conclusively by having the leading witness identify the guilty party at the scene of the crime? I won't go into what he said and how he behaved at the time: his plans for revenge, the names he called her, and the ranting and raving one associates with such crises. I suggested that he try to forget her and at long last devote his attentions to his daughter and his kind loving wife. He agreed to follow my advice, but then he flew into another rage, which eventually gave way to doubt. He began to imagine that Marocas, in order to test his love for her, had contrived the whole thing and had paid Leandro to tell him that story, and the proof was that Leandro had insisted on revealing Marocas' address even after Andrade had made it clear that he wasn't interested in amorous adventures. And clinging to this implausible explanation, Andrade tried to avoid the facts of the situation, but they continued to haunt him: Marocas' pallor, Leandro's sincere happiness, and all the other things that had convinced him that the incident had really taken place. I think he even regretted having carried the matter to such an extreme. After reflecting upon it, I, for my part, could find no explanation for her behavior. She seemed so modest and reserved."

"There's an expression from the theater—by Augier, I think—that could explain the adventure: a longing for the gutter."

"I don't think so, but listen to the rest. At about ten o'clock in the evening, Marocas' maid, an emancipated slave devoted to her mistress, appeared before us in a state of distress. She had been searching for Andrade because Marocas, after hours of weeping behind closed doors, had left home without eating and hadn't returned. I had to restrain Andrade, whose first impulse was to leave at once in search of her. The woman begged us to do everything in our power to find her mistress. 'Doesn't she make a habit of going out?' asked Andrade sarcastically. But the maid said she did not. 'Did you hear that?' he shouted at me. Hope had once again seized hold of the poor devil's heart. 'What about yesterday?' I said. The maid replied that she had gone out the evening before, but I didn't pursue the matter, out of compassion for Andrade, whose grief was increasing and who was swallowing his pride at the thought of losing her. We conducted a search for Marocas and spent the night checking out every place where there was even a remote possibility of finding her. We even went to the police, but our efforts were in vain. The next morning, we returned to the police station. Andrade talked to a friend who was either the chief of police or one of his deputies, revealing only those details of the incident essential for the investigation. His care in withholding certain details was unnecessary, because all his friends were aware of his relationship with Marocas. A complete investigation revealed that no disaster had taken place during the night: none of the boatmen at Praia Grande had heard of a drowning, no firearms or poisons had been sold in the shops. The police brought all their resources to bear on the case but c. .. up empty-handed. I cannot find words to describe Andrade's heartfelt grief during those seemingly endless hours—the whole day had been spent in fruitless search of a clue. He suffered not only from the thought of losing her but also from remorse, doubt, and perhaps a guilty conscience, brought on by the possibility of a disaster, which seemed in his mind to exonerate Marocas. He repeatedly asked me if I, too, would not have reacted as he had in a moment of raging passion. But his suspicions would return, and using arguments just as convincing as those he had used the night before to prove that the incident had never taken place, he would prove Marocas' guilt; he was actually trying to accommodate reality to his feelings at a given moment."

"Did they finally find Marocas?"

"At about eight, when we were having something to eat in a hotel, we received some encouraging news. The evening before, a coachman had taken a lady to a boardinghouse near the Botanical Gardens. We left our food on the table and departed for the Gardens with the coachman. The owner of the boardinghouse confirmed the story, saying that the lady had taken a room the evening before and had eaten nothing since then. She seemed extremely depressed and asked for just a cup of coffee. We went directly to her room, and the owner knocked. She answered in a faint voice and opened the door. Without giving me time to say anything, Andrade pushed me aside, and they fell into one another's arms. After a great deal of weeping, Marocas fainted."

"Did she explain everything?"

"Nothing of the sort. Neither broached the subject again. Once they were saved from the shipwreck, they didn't want to discuss the storm that had almost sent them to the bottom. Harmony was quickly restored. Months later, Andrade bought her a little house in Catumbi. Marocas gave him a son, who died at the age of two. When Andrade went to the North on government business, they were still together, although the fire of their early passion no longer burned with the same intensity. Marocas wanted to accompany him, but I convinced her to stay in Rio. Andrade had intended to return soon, but he passed away in the North. Marocas truly lamented his death, went into mourning, and considered herself a widow. For the first three years of her 'widowhood,' she even attended mass on the anniversary of his death."

"Really, the strangest things do happen—that is, if you haven't taken advantage of my youthful inexperience by inventing the story."

"I haven't invented a thing. It's the honest-to-God truth."

"Well, it's curious. How could she betray him in the middle of such an ardent and sincere affair? I'll stick to my first impression: I think it was a longing for the gutter."

"No. Before then Marocas had never lowered herself to sleeping with the likes of Leandro."

"Then why did she lower herself on that particular night?"

"She was confident there was a social abyss between Leandro and the people she associated with. But chance, which can come in the form of a god or a devil . . . well, it was just one of those things!"

FINAL CHAPTER

Among suicides there is the excellent custom of not departing this life without revealing the motives and circumstances which have armed them against it. Those who leave silently rarely do it out of pride. In most cases, they either do not have time to give an explanation or do not know how to write. It is an excellent idea: in the first place, it's an act of courtesy, as this world is not a ballroom from which a man can sneak away before the cotillion begins. In the second place, the press always gathers and divulges the posthumous letters, and the dead man lives on for a day or two, sometimes a week more.

But in spite of this excellent custom, my original intention was to exit silently. The reason is that after being unlucky all my life, I feared that any last word whatsoever could result in some complication on my way to eternity. But a recent incident changed my plan, and I will retire leaving not just one but two documents. The first one is my will, which I've just finished composing and sealing. It's here on top of my desk, next to the loaded pistol. The second is this autobiographical summary. Note that I'm leaving the second document only because I must clarify the first, which would seem absurd or unintelligible without some additional explanation. In my will, I request that when my few books, clothes, and an old cottage in Catumbi I rent to a carpenter are sold, the proceeds be spent on new shoes and boots, to be distributed in an appropriate manner. I confess that all this is quite extraordinary, and without an explanation for such a legacy the validity of my testament will be questioned. The reason for this legacy grew out of a recent incident which relates to my entire life.

My name is Matias Deodato de Castro e Melo, son of the sergeant Salvador Deodato de Castro e Melo and Dona Maria da Soledade Pereira, both deceased. I am a native of Corumbá, Mato Grosso, and was born on March 3, 1820. Therefore, I am fifty-one years old today, March 3, 1871.

I repeat, I am an unlucky fellow, the most unlucky man in this world. There is an absurd proverbial saying which I literally acted out in Corumbá when I was about seven or eight years old. I was rocking in my hammock at siesta time, in a small room with a tile ceiling. Either because the ends of the hammock were not pulled tightly or because of an overly violent movement on my part, the hammock came loose from one of the walls and I was thrown to the floor. I fell on my back, but even though I was on my back I broke my nose, because a piece of tile which was barely in place and was just waiting for an opportunity to come down took advantage of the confusion and also fell. My wound was neither serious nor long-lived, and thus my father teased me a great deal about it. Father Brito, while drinking *guaraná* with us one afternoon, found out about the episode and cited the proverb, saying I was the first person to literally act out the absurdity of falling on one's back and breaking one's nose. Neither the priest nor my father imagined that this incident was the simple beginning of things to come.

I won't dwell on other misfortunes of my childhood and youth. I want to die at noon, and it's already past eleven. Besides, even though I sent my servant out, he could return earlier than expected and interrupt the execution of my fatal project. If I had time, I'd relate in great detail a whole series of painful episodes, among them a thrashing I received by mistake. The incident involved a rival of a friend of mine, a rival in love, naturally a defeated rival. When my friend and the lady found out about the blows I'd received, they were angered by the rival's treachery, but nevertheless they secretly applauded the fact that I, not my friend, had suffered the beating. I will not speak of certain illnesses I suffered. I'll hasten to the point at which my father, who had been poor all his life, died a pauper. My mother didn't even survive him by two months. Father Brito, who had just been elected to the Chamber of Deputies, offered to take me to Rio de Janeiro with the idea of making me a priest, but he died five days after we arrived. Thus, you can see the constant action of misfortune.

I was left alone at sixteen without friends or resources. A priest from the imperial chapel thought I could become a sacristan there, but due to a lack of openings I wasn't admitted, even though I had served at many masses in Mato Grosso and knew some Latin. Other people convinced me to study law, and I confess I accepted resolutely. At first, I even had some help with my studies. Later, when I was without it, I had to fend for myself but finally managed to earn my law degree. Do not tell me this was an exception to my life of misfortune, for it was my degree that specifically led me into some very painful situations, but as destiny was out to flog me no matter what my profession might be, I attribute no particular surge of bad luck to my degree. It's true that I received it with great pleasure—my youth and a certain superstitious hope for improvement turned that piece of parchment into a diamond key which was to open all the gates of fortune for me.

To begin with, the letter that confirmed my law degree was not the only letter that filled my pockets. No, it had others at its side, ten or fifteen of them, fruits of a love affair contracted in Rio around Easter week of 1842, with a widow seven or eight years older than I, but passionate, sprightly, and well-to-do. She lived on Conde Street with a blind brother—I cannot give out any more information. None of my friends was ignorant of this affair. Two of them even read her letters, which I showed them supposedly so they could admire the widow's elegant style of writing but actually so they could read the exquisite things she said to me. In everyone's opinion, our marriage was a sure thing: the widow was only waiting for me to finish my studies. When I graduated, one of my friends congratulated me, accentuating his conviction with this definitive phrase: "Your marriage is a dogma."

Laughing, he asked me if on account of the dogma, I could lend him five hundred urgently needed dollars. The dogma was still resounding so sweetly in my head that I was unable to rest until I had obtained the money for him. I brought it to him with great enthusiasm, and he received it, full of gratitude. Six months later, he married the widow.

I won't tell you everything I suffered then, I'll only say that my first impulse was to shoot both of them. Mentally, I brought myself to do it. I saw them dying, gasping, begging for my forgiveness. But it was only a hypothetical revenge—in reality, I did nothing. I remained in Rio reading the widow's letters. One of them said: "May God hear me when I say my love is eternal and I'm yours, eternally yours . . ." In my stupefaction, I cursed to myself: "God is jealous. He turned the widow against me because He'll allow no other eternity besides Himself. He turned my friend against me because He'll allow no other dogma besides the Catholic one." That was how I explained the loss of my beloved and the five hundred dollars.

I left the capital and went out into the country to practice law, but not for long. Bad Luck rode behind me on the rear end of the ass, and wherever I dismounted, so did he. I saw his mark in everything—in the cases I did not receive, in the worthless ones I did receive, and in the occasional lucrative ones I invariably lost. Besides the fact that clients who lose are generally less grateful than others, my succession of defeats turned clients away from me. After a year and a half, I returned to Rio and set up a practice with an old classmate, Gonçalves.

I never knew anyone less juridically minded and less apt in confronting legal matters than Gonçalves. Actually, he was a rascal. Let's compare mental activity to an elegant house: Gonçalves couldn't even stand ten minutes of conversation in the parlor—he would slip away, go down to the pantry, and chat with the servants. However, this inferior quality was compensated by a certain lucidity and a quickness to understand less arduous or less complicated matters, as well as an ability to explain and an almost endless supply of cheer, which was quite a blessing for me, a poor devil besieged by misfortune. In the early days, as we received few cases, we killed time with excellent, lively conversation, most of which was his, whether we chatted about politics or women, a subject that was his specialty.

But we finally began to receive some legal cases, among them a dispute over a mortgage. It concerned the house of a customs employee, Temístocles de Sá Botelho, who had no other assets and wanted to save his property. I took charge of the case. Temístocles was delighted with me, and two weeks later, as I had told him I wasn't married, he declared with a laugh that he wanted nothing to do with bachelors. He told me other things and invited me to dine with him the following Sunday. I fell in love with his daughter Rufina, a girl of nineteen, very pretty, but a bit shy and passive. Perhaps it's because of her upbringing, I thought. We were married a few months later. I didn't invite Misfortune, it's true, but inside the church, amid the neat, closely trimmed beards and the lustrous, full sideburns, I thought I saw the sardonic face and oblique glance of my cruel adversary. When the time came to utter the sacred and definitive vows of marriage, that was the reason I trembled and hesitated before I finally stammered out the words the priest dictated to me . . .

So, I was married. True, Rufina was not endowed with brilliant or elegant qualities—for example, she could never have been a sophisticated hostess. However, she did possess adequate domestic qualities, and I did not ask for others. The obscure life was enough for me, and as long as she filled my life, all would go well. But this was precisely the irritating part of the matter. Allow me this chromatic portrait of Rufina: she did not have Cleopatra's black soul, Juliet's blue soul, or Beatrice's white soul, but a dim gray one like most ordinary human beings have. She was kind out of apathy, faithful without virtue, friendly without tenderness. An angel would have taken her to heaven, a demon to hell, effortlessly in either case, for she would not have deserved any particular glory in the first case or acquired the least blemish in the second. She was as passive as a sleepwalker. She was not vain. Our marriage had not taken place at her urging—her father had arranged it so he could have a "doctor" for a son-in-law. She accepted me as she would have accepted a sacristan, a magistrate, a general, a civil servant, or a lieutenant, and she did not do it out of impatience to marry but out of obedience to her family and, to a certain degree, to be like everyone else. All the other women had husbands, so she also wanted to have one. Nothing was more repugnant to my nature, but nevertheless I was married.

Happily—ah! a "happily" in this final chapter in the life of an unlucky man is, in truth, an anomaly, but continue reading and you will see that the adverb belongs to stylistics, not to life; it's a mode of transition, nothing more. What I'm going to relate will not change what has already been said. I'm going to say that Rufina's domestic qualities were great assets. She was modest. She didn't care for dances, walks, or store windows. She kept to herself. She did not work hard at domestic chores, nor was it necessary: I worked to give her everything, and her dresses, hats, and everything else were made by the "French ladies," as seamstresses were called in those days. During the intervals between giving orders, Rufina sat for hours on end, letting her spirit yawn, trying to kill time, a hundred-headed hydra that refused to die. But, I repeat, despite her shortcomings she was a good housewife.

As for me, I played the role of the frogs that wanted a king. The difference is that when Jupiter sent me a log I didn't ask him for another king to replace it, because I knew that if I did, he would send a snake which would come and swallow me. "Three cheers for the log!" I said to myself. I'm only telling you these things so you can see the logic and constancy of my fate.

Another "happily"—and this one is not just a transitional expression. After a year and a half, a hope burst onto the horizon, and judging by the excitement the news gave me, it was a supreme, unique hope. The Desired One was going to arrive. What Desired One? A child. My life changed instantly. Everything smiled on me as if it were a wedding day. I prepared a regal reception for my son. I bought him an expensive cradle of ebony and marble—a finely wrought piece of furniture. Then, piece by piece, I bought his layette: I ordered the finest chambrays, the warmest flannels, and a beautiful ribboned bonnet to be sewn. I bought him a toy cart and waited anxiously, ready to dance before him as David did before the Ark. Oh, misfortune! The Ark arrived empty in Jerusalem, the child was stillborn.

The one who consoled me in my frustration was Gonçalves, who was to have been the child's godfather—he was our friend, regular guest, and confidant. He comforted me and spoke to me of other things with a friend's tenderness. Time did the rest. Gonçalves himself told me later that if the child were to be born as ill-fated as his father, it was better that he had been born dead.

"And you think he wouldn't have been?" I retorted.

Gonçalves smiled—he didn't believe in my chronic misfortune. The truth is that he didn't have time to believe in anything, for he devoted all his time and energy to being happy. But finally he had begun to devote himself to his legal career. He now defended clients, drafted petitions, and attended hearings, all because he had to live, he said. And he was always happy. My wife thought he was charming and laughed heartily at his sayings and stories, which were overly risqué at times. At first I reproached him privately because of his anecdotes, but eventually I grew accustomed to them. And besides, is there anyone who can't forgive the frivolity of a jovial friend? I must say that at one point Gonçalves himself began to subdue his behavior, and from then on I began to see great seriousness in him. "You're in love," I told him one day, and he, turning pale, answered yes and added with a smile, though a weak one, that marriage was indispensable. At the dinner table I spoke about the matter.

"Rufina, do you know that Gonçalves is going to get married?"

"It's a joke of his," Gonçalves interrupted quickly.

I told my indiscretion to go to the devil and didn't mention the subject again—neither did he. Five months later . . . the transition is brief, but there is no way to lengthen it: Rufina fell ill, seriously ill, and didn't even last a week. She died of a malign fever.

Strange thing: in life, the differences in our temperaments had weakened the ties between us, which in any case had been maintained primarily out of necessity and habit. Death, with its great spiritual power, transformed everything—Rufina appeared to me as the wife who descends from Lebanon, and the differences between us were replaced by a total fusion of our beings. I seized the image, which filled my entire soul, and with it filled my entire life, where it formerly had occupied so little space for such a short time. I was making an act of defiance against my evil star by constructing a building of good fortune in solid, indestructible rock. Understand me well. Until then everything which had depended on the external world had been naturally precarious: tiles fell with the swaying of hammocks, ecclesiastical robes rebelled against the sacristans, widows' vows fled with friends' dogmas, legal cases came erratically or disappeared instantly, and, finally, children were born dead. But the image of the dead woman was immortal, and with it I could defy the oblique glance of Evil Destiny. Happiness was held captive in my hands and, like a condor, was beating its huge wings in the air while Misfortune, like an owl, flapped its wings and headed off toward night and silence . . .

However, one day when I was convalescing from a fever, I decided to make an inventory of some of my wife's possessions and began with a small box, which had not been opened since her death, five months earlier. I found a multitude of minuscule items: needles, thread, sewing inserts, a thimble, a pair of scissors, a prayer by Saint Cyprian, a roll of cloth, other odds and ends, and a bundle of letters held together by a blue ribbon. I untied the ribbon and opened the letters: they were from Gonçalves . . . Noon already! I must finish. The servant will return soon, and my plans will be ruined. No one can imagine how time slips by under these circumstances: minutes fly by as if they were empires, and, more important, sheets of paper are just as quickly covered with words.

I won't dwell on all the worthless lottery tickets, aborted business deals, interrupted communications, or other spiteful acts of fate. Tired and annoyed, I realized I could not find happiness anywhere. I even went beyond that: I came to believe it did not exist anywhere on earth, and consequently I've been preparing myself since yesterday for my great plunge into eternity. Today I had breakfast, smoked a cigar, and leaned out the window. After ten minutes had gone by, I saw a well-dressed man who frequently stared down at his feet as he walked. I knew him by sight—he was a victim of great reversals of fortune, but he was nevertheless happily walking along contemplating his feet, or rather his shoes. They were new, of patent leather, very well cut, and probably sewn with great care. He looked up toward the windows and toward people but always looked back down at his shoes, as if by a law of attraction that preceded and was superior to will. He was happy—one could see the expression of bliss on his face. He was obviously happy, even though he might not have eaten any breakfast and didn't have a cent in his pockets. But he was happy and contemplated his boots.

Could happiness be a pair of boots? This man, so buffeted about by life, has finally received a smile from fortune. This man is oblivious to everything except his shoes. No preoccupation of this century, no social or moral problem, none of the new generation's joys or the old one's sorrows, no form of misery, class war, or political or artistic crisis—none of these things is worth a pair of boots. He stares at them, breathes them, shines along with them, treads along with them upon the soil of a planet that belongs to him. Hence, the pride in his stance, the firmness of his steps, and a certain air of Olympic tranquility . . . Yes, happiness is a pair of boots.

There is no other explanation for my will. The superficial readers will say I'm insane, that my delirium is evident in every clause of the testament, but I'm speaking to the wise and the unfortunate. It is not valid to object that it would be better to spend on myself the money I intend to spend on boots, for in that case I would be the only beneficiary. By distributing the boots, I'll make a certain number of people happy. Cheer up, unlucky people of the world! May my final wish be granted! Good night, and put your shoes on!

A SECOND LIFE

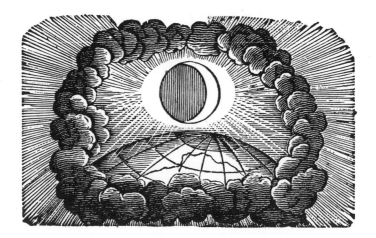

Monsignor Caldas interrupted the stranger's narration: "Will you excuse me? I'll be back in a moment."

He stood up, went to the interior of the house, called his old Negro servant, and said to him in a low voice: "João, go over to the police station, speak to the captain for me, and ask him to come here with one or two men to take a madman off my hands. Go on, hurry." And returning to the room: "Ready," he said, "we can continue."

"As I was saying, I died on March 20, 1860, at 5:43 in the morning. I was then sixty-eight years old. My soul flew through space until it lost sight of the earth, leaving the moon, sun, and stars far below. It finally penetrated an empty space which was only dimly illuminated. I continued to rise and began to see a tiny dot shining brightly, very far off in the distance. The point grew larger and became a sun. I entered it without burning, because souls are incombustible. Has yours ever caught fire?"

"No, sir."

"They are incombustible. I kept rising. At one point I heard some delightful music coming from a distance of about 40,000 leagues, and when

I was 5,000 leagues away from it, a throng of souls descended and carried me away on a litter of ether and feathers. Shortly thereafter, I entered the new sun, which is the planet of the virtuous souls of the earth. I'm not a poet, Monsignor, so I don't dare describe to you the magnificence of that divine abode. Even if I were a poet, I couldn't convey to you with human language the feeling of greatness, splendor, happiness, and ecstasy, or the melodies and flashes of light and colors, all of which are indefinable and incomprehensible. You would have to see it to believe it. Once inside, I found out that my arrival marked the completion of another group of one thousand souls—that was the reason for the extraordinary celebrations they gave in my honor, which lasted two centuries or, by our meas- urements, forty-eight hours. Finally, after the celebrations ended, they in- vited me to return to earth to live a new life—it was the privilege granted to each thousandth soul. I answered with gratitude and refused, but refusal was not allowed. It was an eternal law. The only liberty they gave me was the choice of the vehicle: I could be born a prince or a coach driver. What was I to do? What would you have done in my place?"

"I don't know, it depends . . ."

"You're right, it depends on the circumstances. But imagine that mine were such that it wouldn't be pleasant for me to return here. I was the victim of inexperience, Monsignor, and for that reason I had been unhappy in my old age. I remembered always hearing my father and other older people say when they saw a young boy: 'How I wish I were that young again, knowing what I know now!' After remembering this, I declared that it made no difference whether I was born a beggar or a potentate, as long as I could be born experienced. You can't imagine the universal laughter with which they heard me. Job, who presides over the province of the patient, told me that such a wish was ridiculous, but I persisted and won. Shortly thereafter, I was gliding through space. I spent nine months getting here, and then I fell into the arms of a wet nurse and named myself José Maria. Your first name is Romualdo, isn't it?"

"Yes, sir—Romualdo de Sousa Caldas."

"Might you be related to Father Sousa Caldas?"

"No, sir."

"A great poet, Father Caldas. Poetry is a gift, I could never even com- pose ten lines. But let's get to the heart of the matter. First I'll tell you what happened to me, then I'll tell you what I need to ask of you, Monsignor. Meanwhile, if you'll allow me to smoke . . ."

Monsignor Caldas made a gesture of assent without losing sight of the cane that lay across José Maria's lap. José Maria slowly rolled a cigarette. He was a little over thirty years old, pale, with a look sometimes gentle and somber, at other times agitated and explosive. He had appeared after the priest had finished lunch and asked for an audience regarding a serious and urgent matter. Monsignor Caldas had him come inside and sit down. After ten minutes, he realized the man was a lunatic. He excused the incoherence of his ideas and the astonishing aspects of his inventions, for he could perhaps use them as material for a study. However, the stranger had had a fit of anger that frightened the peaceable cleric. How could he and his servant, both of them old, defend themselves against any act of aggression from a powerful, crazed man? While he awaited the aid of the police, Monsignor Caldas was all smiles and nods, was frightened along with him, happy along with him—useful politics with madmen, women, and potentates. José Maria finally lit his cigarette and continued his story:

"I was reborn on January 5, 1861. I can't tell you anything about my second infancy, because during this period experience is only of an instinctive form. I suckled very little and cried as little as possible in order not to be punished. For fear of falling, I began to walk late—hence, my legs are a bit weak. Fearing bruises and blood, I never did any of such useful things as running, tumbling, climbing trees, jumping over fences, and exchanging punches. Frankly, I had a tedious childhood, and school was no exception. Everyone called me a fool and a sissy. In fact, I lived by running away from everything. I don't believe I ever slipped during my childhood, but neither did I ever run. Word of honor, it was a very difficult time, and as I compare the bumps and bruises of those days with the tedium of today, I prefer the bumps and bruises. I grew up, I became a young man, I entered a period of romance . . . Don't be alarmed. I'll be chaste, as I was at my first supper. Do you know what a supper between young men and ladies of easy virtue is like?"

"How do you expect me to know?"

"I was twenty," continued José Maria, "and you can't imagine the astonishment of my friends when I declared I was ready to go to such a supper . . . No one expected such a thing of such a cautious youth, who ran from everything—from insufficient sleep, excessive sleep, walking alone in the wee hours of the morning—and who lived, so to speak, groping his way through the darkness. I went to the supper, at the Botanical Gardens, a splendid setting. Food, wine, lights, flowers, cheerful youths, ladies with charming eyes, and, above all, the appetite of a twenty-year-old. Can you believe I didn't eat anything? The memory of three cases of indigestion I had suffered in my first life, forty years earlier, made me refrain. I lied, saying I wasn't feeling well. One of the ladies came and sat at my right, to cure me, and another came and sat at my left, with the same intention. 'You cure one side and I'll cure the other,' they said to each other. They were cheerful, fresh, wily, with a reputation for devouring young men's hearts and lives. I confess that I became fearful and withdrawn. They did everything possible to cheer me up, but all their efforts were in vain. I left in the morning, enamored of both of them, but without having won either, and I was faint from hunger. What do you think?" asked José Maria, placing his hands on his knees and turning his elbows outward.

"As a matter of fact . . ."

"I won't tell you anything more, you can guess the rest. My second life is like an expansive and impetuous youth, inhibited by a basically traditional experience. I'm like Eurico, tied to my own cadaver[1] . . . no, that's not a good comparison. What do you think my life is like?"

"I'm not very imaginative. I suppose you live like a great big bird with its legs tied together, that flaps its wings like this . . ."

José Maria got up and waved his arms as if they were wings. As he stood up, his cane fell to the floor, but he did not attempt to retrieve it. He continued to wave his arms about as he stood facing the priest and said he was precisely that, a huge bird . . . Every time he beat his arms against his thighs he stood up on his toes, moving his body in a rhythmic cadence, and he held his feet together, to show they were bound. Monsignor nodded his approval, but at the same time he tuned his ears so as to be able to hear any footsteps on the stairway. Everything was silent. All he heard was noise from the outside: carriages and wagons going down the street, street vendors shouting their wares, someone in the neighborhood playing the piano. After picking up his cane, José Maria finally sat down and continued his story:

"A bird, a great big bird. To see how appropriate the comparison is, the adventure that brought me here will suffice—a matter of conscience, a passion, a woman, a widow, Dona Clemência. She's twenty-six, has a pair of eyes that are infinite, not in size, but in expression, and, above them, two dabs of down which complete her facial features. She's the daughter of a retired professor. Black dresses are so becoming to her that sometimes I tell her she became a widow only to be able to wear mourning. It's only a joke! We met a year ago, at the home of a rancher from Cantagalo. We left the place in love with one another. I already know what you're going to ask me: why didn't we get married, since we were both free to do so?"

"Yes, why didn't you?"

1. Eurico, protagonist of *Eurico, O Presbítero* (*Euric, the Presbyter*) a novel by the Portuguese novelist, poet, and historian Alexandre Herculano (1810–1877). When Eurico is reunited with his beloved after a ten-year separation, he tells her he spent the last ten years "tied to his own cadaver."—Trans.

"But, man of God! That is precisely the subject of my adventure. We were free, we cared for each other, and we weren't going to get married— such is the predicament I've come to explain to you, which will perhaps be solved by your theology, or whatever it is. We returned to Rio as sweethearts. Clemência was living with her elderly father and a brother employed in commerce. I introduced myself to both of them and began to call on them at their home in Matacavalos. Furtive glances, hand holding, some disconnected words, others connected, a sentence here, two sentences there, and then we confessed our love to each other. One night on the staircase landing, we kissed for the first time . . . Excuse the details, Monsignor, keep in mind that you're hearing my confession. I'm only telling you this to let you know why I went away dumfounded, in a daze, with the image of Clemência in my head and the savor of her kiss in my mouth. I roamed for nearly two hours planning an idyllic future. I decided I would ask for her hand at the end of the week and marry her a month later. I even imagined the final details, composing and embellishing the wedding announcements in my head. I got home after midnight, and then the picture I had imagined of our life together flew away like a set change in an old theater piece. Can you guess how it happened?"

"I can't imagine . . ."

"It occurred to me as I was removing my waistcoat that our love might end soon . . . it does happen sometimes. As I took off my boots, I thought of something worse—we could grow tired of each other. I concluded my evening toilette, lit a cigarette, and as I lay back on the settee, thought that routine and familiarity could save everything. But soon afterward I realized that our dispositions might be incompatible, and what could be done about two incompatible but inseparable dispositions? But finally, since our passion was so strong and violent, I dismissed all these doubts and imagined myself married, the father of a beautiful child . . . Just one? Two, three, eight, even ten could arrive, some of them crippled. Or a crisis or two could arise—lack of money, destitution, illness, or one of those spurious dalliances that disturb domestic peace . . . I considered everything and concluded it would be best not to get married. What I can't describe to you is my despair—there are no words to describe what I suffered that night . . . Do you mind if I smoke another cigarette?"

He didn't wait for an answer, but went ahead and rolled his cigarette, then lit it. Monsignor Caldas could not help marveling at his handsome head, such a contrast to his disordered mental condition. At the same time, he noted that the stranger spoke in refined terms and was well mannered in spite of his morbid outbursts. Who in the world could this man be? José Maria continued his story, saying that he stayed away from

Clemência's house for six days, but he couldn't resist her letters or her tears. After a week he ran to her and confessed everything. She listened to him with great interest, wishing to know how she could put an end to so many doubts and what proof of love he wanted her to give him. José Maria's answer was a question.

" 'Are you willing to make a great sacrifice for me?' I asked her. Clemência swore she would. 'Well, then, leave everything, family and society, come and live with me. We'll get married after this novitiate.' I can see your eyes are growing wide. Hers filled with tears, but despite her humiliation, she agreed to everything. Go on, tell me I'm a monster."

"No, sir . . ."

"Why not? I'm a monster. Clemência came to my house, and you can't imagine how happy I was to see her. 'I'm leaving everything, you're the universe to me,' she said. I kissed her feet, I kissed the heels of her shoes. You can't imagine my contentment. The next day I received a letter bordered in black, news of the death of an uncle of mine in Santa Ana do Livramento, leaving me $20,000. I was astonished. 'I understand,' I said to Clemência, 'you sacrificed everything because you had heard about the inheritance.' This time Clemência didn't cry, she got up and left. I ran after her, ashamed, begging for her forgiveness, but she refused. One, two, three days went by, but all my efforts were in vain. Clemência refused to yield; she wouldn't even speak. Then I declared I would kill myself. I bought a revolver, went to her, and showed it to her—it's this one."

Monsignor Caldas grew pale. José Maria showed him the revolver for a few seconds, then he put it back in his pocket and continued.

"I fired a shot. Frightened, she took the gun away from me and forgave me. We decided to marry as soon as possible, but I imposed one condition: I would donate the $20,000 to the National Library. Clemência flung herself into my arms and showed her approval with a kiss. I gave away the $20,000—you must have read about it in the newspapers . . . Three weeks later we were married. You're sighing, as if you think I've reached the end. Nonsense! Now we reach the tragic part of the story. I can abbreviate some details and eliminate others, but I'll limit myself to Clemência. I won't speak to you about all my other mutilated emotions, aborted pleasures, plans that came apart in mid-air, shattered illusions, nor will I speak about that bird." . . . flap . . . flap . . . flap . . .

And with a leap José Maria was once again on his feet, flailing his arms about and moving his body in cadence. Monsignor Caldas' sweat ran cold. After a few seconds, José Maria stopped, sat down, and resumed his narration, now less coherent, more furious, obviously more delirious. He told of the fear, misery, and suspicion in which he lived. He could no longer nibble at a fig, as before: his fear of finding an insect inside reduced its flavor. He was suspicious of the happy expressions of people in the streets because preoccupations, desires, hate, sadness, and other things were disguised by three-fourths of them. He lived in fear of fathering a blind, deaf-mute, or tubercular child or a potential assassin. He could not give a dinner that would not become gloomy soon after the soup was finished, because of the idea that something he or his wife might say or do, or anything lacking in the service, might cause his guests to spread rumors about him out in the street beneath a lamppost. Experience had given him the terror of being ridiculed. He confessed to Monsignor that in reality, he had never gained anything in his life. On the contrary, he had lost, for he had been driven to blood . . . He was going to tell Monsignor about the blood. The previous night he had gone to bed early and dreamed . . . Whom did Monsignor think he had dreamed about?

"I can't imagine . . ."

"I dreamed the Devil was reading the Gospel to me. As he neared the point at which Christ speaks of the lilies of the field, the Devil picked a few and gave them to me. 'Take them,' he said, 'they are the lilies of the Scriptures. As you know, even Solomon in all his glory was not arrayed like one of these. Solomon is wisdom. Do you know what these lilies are, José Maria? They are your twenty years.' I stared at them, enchanted—they were more beautiful than one could ever imagine. The Devil took hold of the lilies, sniffed them, and told me to sniff them too. You won't believe what happened next: as soon as I lifted them up to my nose, I saw a repulsive, foul-smelling reptile emerge from inside them—I cried out and flung the lilies far from me. Then the Devil, breaking out into a formidable guffaw, said: 'José Maria, they are your twenty years.' It was a belly laugh like this: ha, ha, ha, ha, ha . . ."

José Maria laughed without restraint in a strident, diabolical manner. Suddenly, he stopped. He stood up and said that as soon as he opened his eyes he saw his wife standing before him, anguished and disheveled. Clemência's eyes were sweet, but he told her that gentle eyes can also do harm. She threw herself at his feet . . . At this point, José Maria's expression was so frenzied that the priest, also on his feet, began to back away from him, pale and trembling. "No, you wretch! No! You won't get away from me!" bellowed José Maria as he headed toward him. His eyes were bulging out of their sockets, his temples palpitating, the priest was backing away . . . backing away . . . Coming up the staircase a shuffling of swords and feet was heard.

DONA PAULA

She couldn't possibly have arrived at a more opportune time. Dona Paula entered the parlor precisely as her niece was drying her tear-swollen eyes. She was surprised, as was her niece Venancinha, who knew that her aunt rarely descended from the Tijuca district, where she lived. It was May 1882, and Venancinha hadn't seen her aunt since Christmas. Dona Paula had come down the previous day to spend the night with her sister on Lavradio Street. Today, she had dressed and run off to visit her niece right after lunch. A slave who saw her wanted to announce her arrival, but Dona Paula told her not to—to avoid rustling her skirts, she tiptoed ever so slowly to the parlor door, opened it, and went in.

"What's this all about?" she exclaimed.

Flinging herself into Dona Paula's arms, Venancinha burst into tears. Her aunt kissed, embraced, and comforted her and insisted that she tell her what the matter was. Was she sick, or . . .

"I wish to God I were sick! Death would be better!" interrupted the girl.

"Don't talk nonsense! What happened? Come now, tell me."

Venancinha dried her eyes and tried to talk. After five or six words, the tears flowed again, in such abundance and with such force that Dona Paula thought she'd best wait until they subsided. Meanwhile, she took off her black lace mantelet and her gloves. She was a striking, elegant woman with large attractive eyes that must have been irresistible when she was younger. While her niece wept, she moved quietly to close the parlor door, then returned to the settee. After a few minutes, Venancinha stopped crying and told her aunt what had happened.

It was nothing less than a quarrel with her husband, so violent they had even spoken of separating. Jealousy had caused it. For some time her husband had been suspicious of a certain gentleman, but the evening before, after seeing his wife dance with the man twice and talk to him for a few minutes, he concluded they were in love. When they returned home he was sullen. The next morning after breakfast, he exploded and said cruel harsh things, which she answered in kind.

"Where's your husband now?" inquired her aunt.

"He's gone. I think he went to the office."

Dona Paula asked her if his office were still in the same building and told her not to worry; it wasn't a serious matter. Within two hours everything would be settled. She quickly put on her gloves.

"Are you going there, Auntie?"

"Going there? Of course I'm going! Your husband's a good man—it was just a lover's quarrel. Number 104? I'm on my way, and don't let the slaves see you looking like this!"

Dona Paula spoke with volubility, self-assurance, and kindness. She put on her gloves, and Venancinha, as she helped her aunt with her mantelet, swore she adored Conrad despite their quarrel. Conrad, her husband, had been practicing law since 1874. As Dona Paula left, her niece showered her with kisses of gratitude. In all truth, she couldn't possibly have arrived at a more opportune time. On her way to see Conrad, Dona Paula reflected upon the incident with curiosity, if not suspicion, a little uneasy as to what the whole truth of the matter might be. In any case, she was determined to restore domestic peace.

When she reached her nephew's office, he was not yet in, but shortly thereafter he arrived. After his initial surprise at seeing her there, he guessed the object of her visit. He confessed that he had overreacted with his wife and said he was not accusing her of loose morals or perverse intentions. But she was behaving like a scatterbrain: she was too friendly with other men and was given to coquettish glances and honeyed words in their presence. And indiscretion was one of the gateways to misconduct. Furthermore, he had no doubt that his wife and the man in question were in love with one another. Venancinha had only told her about the evening before—she had not mentioned four or five other incidents, one of which had occurred at the theater and had developed into a scandal of sorts. He wasn't about to accept the responsibility for his wife's reckless and indiscreet behavior. If she wanted to go around falling in love, she'd have to pay the price for it.

Dona Paula heard him out. Then it was her turn to speak. She agreed that her niece was flighty but attributed this to her youth. A pretty girl could not help attracting attention, and it was natural for Venancinha to be flattered by the admiring glances of other men. It was also understandable that her response to such flattery was interpreted as a sign of love, by other men as well as her husband—their infatuation and his jealousy were the cause of the quarrel. She, for her part, had just seen her niece crying in earnest. When she left, Venancinha was disconsolate and brokenhearted and had even talked of wanting to die because of what he had said to her. So if he really only attributed her actions to foolishness, why not proceed with discretion and understanding? He should use counsel and common sense—he could help her avoid similar situations in the future and show her how even the appearance of friendship and good will toward other men could be misinterpreted and harm her reputation.

The good lady spoke no less than twenty minutes, and she expressed herself so eloquently and diplomatically that her nephew felt his heart softening. He resisted, of course—two or three times, to avoid appearing overly lenient, he declared that everything between them was finished. In self-justification, he mentally evoked his arguments against a reconciliation. But Dona Paula looked down until his wave of indignation had passed and then looked up at him with her large, sagacious, imploring eyes.

Seeing that Conrad wasn't going to give in easily, Dona Paula proposed a compromise: "Forgive her, and make your peace together, then I'll take her to Tijuca to spend a month or two with me. It will be a kind of temporary exile for her. Meanwhile, I'll take it upon myself to straighten her out. Agreed?"

Conrad accepted. As soon as Dona Paula had his word, she prepared to leave to tell her niece the encouraging news. Conrad accompanied her to the stairs, where they shook hands. Dona Paula didn't release his hand until she had repeated her recommendation that he proceed with tenderness and discretion. Then, as though it were an afterthought, she added: "And you're going to see that the man in question isn't worth even a minute of the time we've spent worrying over him."

"His name is Vasco Maria Portela."

Dona Paula turned pale. What Vasco Maria Portela? An elderly gentleman, a former diplomat who . . . no, he was retired, had been in Europe for a few years, and had just received the title of baron. It was his son, a worthless rascal who had returned to Rio from Europe a short time before. Dona Paula squeezed Conrad's hand and hurried downstairs. Confused and excited, she spent several minutes at the landing going through the motions of adjusting her mantelet. She stared at the floor, pondering the situation. Then she set out to meet her niece, carrying with her the proposal for a reconciliation with Conrad and the conditions under which it was to be achieved. Venancinha accepted everything.

Two days later, they went to Dona Paula's home in the Tijuca district. If Venancinha seemed to have lost some of her earlier enthusiasm for the trip, the loss was probably due to the idea of exile or to longing for what she had left behind. In any event, Vasco's name went up to Tijuca. If it wasn't in both heads, it was at least in Dona Paula's, where it was a kind of echo, a remote and pleasant sound, something that seemed to hearken from the time of the opera singer Stoltz and the Marquis of Paraná. Those distant echoes were just as fragile as youth itself, and where were those three eternities now? They were scattered among the distant ruins of the past thirty years. Dona Paula, having nothing else to look forward to, lived with those memories of the past.

The elder Vasco had also been young once and had loved. Unbeknown to their marriage partners, he and Dona Paula had filled their cups to the brim and for several years had slaked their thirst for one another. Since the passing winds are unable to record men's speeches, there is no way to reveal here what was said at the time about their adventure, which eventually came to an end. It had been a series of sweet and bitter hours mixed with pleasures and tears, ecstasy and anger, and various other intoxicants the lady had used when she filled her loving cup to overflowing. She drained the cup dry and never touched it again. Satiety was followed by abstinence, and public opinion was formed by this final phase. Her husband died and the years flowed by. Dona Paula was now an austere and pious lady, prestigious and respected by all.

Dona Paula's thought had been carried to the past by her niece. The two similar situations, mingled with the same name and blood, awakened some old memories. They were going to be living together in Tijuca for a few weeks, and Venancinha would be following her aunt's instructions. Dona Paula would attempt to challenge her own memory—to what extent could she reexperience those sensations from the past?

"Aren't we going to the city at all? Not even for a little visit?" asked Venancinha the next morning, laughing.

"Are you bored already?"

"No, I'd never be bored here, I was just asking if . . ."

Dona Paula, also laughing, shook her finger negatively. Then she asked her niece if she missed the city. Venancinha said no and gave more weight to her answer by allowing the corners of her mouth to droop, in order to reflect her disdain or indifference. It was as though she had written a letter saying more than she had intended to say. Avoiding the reckless abandon of someone rushing off to save his father from the hangman's noose, Dona Paula had the good habit of reading slowly. She fixed her attention on the spaces between the letters and the lines, took in everything, and found her niece's response excessive.

"They're in love with one another," she thought.

This discovery awakened her dormant memories of the past. Dona Paula struggled to shake off those persistent memories, but they returned like a group of chorus girls: some slowly and suggestively, others with quick and sprightly movements—they sang, laughed, and raised the very devil. Dona Paula's mind returned to the dances of yesteryear. She remembered the eternal waltzes that made everyone stare at her in wonder and boasted to her niece about the mazurkas, the most graceful dance in the world, the theater, cardgames, and, obliquely, the kisses. But everything—and this was the curious thing about her recollections— everything was described with the cold and faded ink of an old chronicle, an empty skeleton of history that lacked a living soul. Everything occurred in her head. Dona Paula tried synchronizing her heart and her head to see if she could feel something beyond a mere mental reproduction of her past, but despite all efforts to evoke the old feelings, none returned. Time had swallowed them.

If she could only peek into her niece's heart, she might be able to see her own image reflected there, and then . . . After Dona Paula was possessed by this idea, it became harder for her to concentrate on her niece's rehabilitation, even though she was sincerely preoccupied with her welfare and wanted to see her reunited with Conrad. In order to assure themselves of company in purgatory, habitual sinners may secretly desire to see others committing sins too, but sinning wasn't the issue here. Dona Paula stressed Conrad's virtues and superiority and also told her niece that uncontrolled passions could destroy her marriage and, even more tragic, cause her husband to disown her.

Conrad confirmed the validity of Dona Paula's warnings when he paid his first visit nine days later: he was cold when he entered and when he left. Venancinha was terrified. She had hoped that their nine-day separation would soften her husband, and, really, it had. But in order to avoid the appearance of an easy capitulation, he masked his true feelings and held back his emotions. And this had a greater effect than anything else. Venancinha's terrible fear of losing her husband was the principal factor in her rehabilitation. Exile alone could not have accomplished so much.

Just two days after Conrad's visit, when both ladies had approached the villa gate to set out on their daily stroll, they saw a gentleman on horseback coming in their direction. Venancinha fixed her eyes on him, let out a little cry, and ran to hide behind the wall. Dona Paula understood and waited. She wanted to see the man close-up. After two or three minutes he approached. Seated upright in his saddle, he was a handsome, proud-looking, elegant youth with fine polished boots. He looked just like the other Vasco—the same large deep-set eyes, the same tilt of the head, the same broad shoulders.

After Dona Paula had pried the first word out of her niece, Venancinha told her everything that very night. They had first seen one another at the horse races, right after his return from Europe. Two weeks later, she was introduced to him at a dance. He seemed so interesting and Parisian that she spoke to her husband about him the next morning. Conrad frowned in displeasure, and this reaction gave her an idea she had never before entertained. She began to see him with pleasure, and then she longed to see him. He spoke to her respectfully and told her nice things: that she was the loveliest and most elegant young woman in Rio, that in Paris he had recently heard some ladies from the Alvarenga family praising her fine qualities. He was witty when he criticized other people and expressed himself more sensitively than anyone she had ever met. He didn't talk about love, but he pursued her with his eyes—no matter how hard she tried to look away from him, she couldn't help noticing. She began to think about him, frequently and with interest, and her heart fluttered whenever they met. It was probably easy for him to detect in her face the impression he made.

Leaning forward, Dona Paula listened to Venancinha's story with her whole past concentrated in her eyes. With mouth agape, she seemed anxious to drink in her niece's words, as if they were a cordial. And she asked for more, telling Venancinha to omit nothing whatsoever. Dona Paula looked so youthful and her request was so gentle and full of potential forgiveness that she seemed like a confidant and friend, despite a few harsh words interspersed among the pleasant remarks through a sort of unconscious hypocrisy. It wasn't intentional, however: Dona Paula even deceived herself. She was like an invalid general who struggles to recover some of his old ardor by listening to the stories of another's campaigns.

"You can see your husband was right," she said. "You were foolish, very foolish."

Venancinha agreed with her aunt and swore it was completely finished.
"I'm afraid it isn't. Did you really come to love him?"

"Auntie . . ."

"You still love him!"

"I swear I don't love him anymore, but I . . . yes, I confess I did. Forgive
me, and please don't say anything to Conrad! I wish none of this had ever
happened. Yes, I'll admit I was smitten at first . . . But what did you expect?"

"Did he reveal his feelings to you?"

"Yes, he did. It happened at the Lyric Theater one evening, as we were
about to leave. He usually came by my theater box to accompany me to
the carriage, and on our way out he uttered . . . three words."

Out of consideration, Dona Paula didn't ask for the gentleman's words,
but she imagined the circumstances: the galleries, the couples leaving, the
lights, the crowds, the sound of voices, and the scene she visualized allowed her to piece together some of the sensations her niece had experienced. With great interest and diplomacy, she asked her to describe her
feelings in greater detail.

"I don't know exactly what I felt," replied Venancinha, her tongue gradually loosened by her growing emotion. "I don't remember the first five
minutes. I think I maintained my dignity—in any event, I didn't answer him.
I felt that everyone was staring at us, that they might have overheard him,
and when people greeted me with a smile it seemed that they were mock-
ing me. Somehow I managed to go down the stairs and without really
knowing what I was doing, got into the carriage. I allowed my fingers to go
limp when we shook hands good-by. I can assure you that I wish I hadn't
heard anything he said. When we were inside the carriage, Conrad told me
he was tired and leaned back against the far side of the seat. It was for the
best, because I don't know what I would have said if we had talked on the
way home. I leaned back too, but not for long—I wasn't able to sit still. I
looked out the glass windows, and from time to time I could see only the
glare of streetlamps, and then not even that. Instead I saw the theater
galleries, the stairs, the crowds of people, and him next to me whispering
those words, just three words, and I'm not able to say what I thought
then—my ideas were jumbled and confused, and I felt a churning inside
me."

"But after you were back home?"

"At home, as I undressed, I was at last able to reflect a little, but very little.
I slept poorly and late. The next morning I was bewildered. I cannot say I
was happy or sad. I remember I thought about him a lot, and to get him

out of my mind, I promised myself I would reveal everything to Conrad, but the thoughts returned again. From time to time I shuddered, imagining I heard his voice. Then I remembered that when I gave him my hand my fingers were limp, and I felt—I don't know exactly how to say it—a kind of regret, a fear of having offended him. Then I wanted to see him again . . . Forgive me, Auntie, but you asked me to tell everything."

Dona Paula's answer was a tight squeeze of the hand and an understanding nod. Through these ingenuously narrated sensations, she had at last found something from her own past. Sometimes, in a dreamy trance of reminiscence, her eyelids were half-closed; at other times her eyes were sparkling with warmth and curiosity. She heard everything: day by day and encounter by encounter, including the details of the scene in the theater, which her niece had initially hidden from her. And the rest followed: the hours of anxiety, longing, fear, hope, depression, and dissimulation, all the deeply felt emotions of a young girl in this situation. To satisfy her insatiable curiosity, Dona Paula insisted on knowing every detail of her niece's story, which was neither a book nor even a chapter of adultery, but a prolog, interesting and violent.

Venancinha finished. Her aunt, in a state of rapture, said nothing. Then she came to, took her niece by the hand, and drew her closer. She didn't talk right away. First she stared intently at her niece's deep-set eyes, fresh mouth, and restless, palpitating youthfulness. She wasn't drawn entirely out of her trance until Venancinha once again begged her forgiveness. Dona Paula said everything with a mother's tenderness and austerity. She spoke so eloquently of chastity, public opinion, and loving one's husband that Venancinha wept, unable to contain herself.

Tea was served, but it wasn't really an appropriate time for tea. Venancinha retired immediately—as it was still quite light, she left the room with her eyes lowered so the servant wouldn't see her in such a state of emotion. Dona Paula remained seated at the table, in the presence of the servant. She spent about twenty minutes drinking her tea and munching on a biscuit. As soon as she was alone, she went to lean against the window which looked out from the back of the villa.

The wind blew gently and the leaves rustled with a whispering sound. Although they weren't the leaves of her youth, they nevertheless questioned her: "Paula, do you remember the leaves of yesteryear?" For that is the peculiar thing about leaves: the generations that pass on tell the newcomers what they saw, and that is why all leaves know and ask questions about everything. "Do you remember the leaves of yesteryear?"

She did remember, of course, but that sensation she had felt a short time before, which was scarcely a reverberation, had ceased. In vain she repeated her niece's words as she breathed in the pungent evening air, but instead of recapturing sensations from the past, she was only able to evoke the scattered lifeless reminiscences in her head. Her heart slowed down, and her blood ran at its normal speed again. When her niece was absent she felt nothing. Nonetheless, she stayed there, staring out at the night, which had nothing in common with the nights of Stoltz and the Marquis of Paraná. But she stared out anyway, and in the kitchen the slave women fought off their drowsiness by telling stories. Now and then they commented impatiently, "Seems like the old missus ain't never going to bed tonight!"

THE DIPLOMAT

The servant girl entered the dining room, went up to the table that was surrounded by people, and spoke softly to her mistress. It must have been something urgent, because the lady of the house got up immediately.

"Shall we wait, Dona Adelaide?"

"No, don't wait, Senhor Rangel, keep on playing. I'll be back later."

Rangel was the reader of the book of fortunes. He turned the page and read off a title: "Does someone love you secretly?" There was movement in the room, and young ladies and gentlemen smiled at one another. It was Saint John's Night, 1854, and the house was on Mangueira Street. The host's name was João Viegas, and he had a daughter, Joaninha. Every year the same group of friends and relatives got together, a bonfire was burned in the backyard, potatoes were roasted, and fortunes were read. There was also a dinner, sometimes a dance or parlor games, and the mood was very informal and friendly. João Viegas was a clerk at a civil court in Rio.

"Let's continue. Whose turn is it now?" he said. It must be Dona Felismina's. Let's see if someone loves you secretly."

Dona Felismina smiled halfheartedly. She was fortyish, devout, neither talented nor rich, and spent her life searching for a husband. In truth, the joke was a bit cruel, though appropriate. Dona Felismina was the epitome of those indulgent, gentle creatures who seem to have been born to amuse others. She picked up the dice and threw them with an air of incredulous affability. "Number ten!" shouted two voices. Rangel lowered his eyes to the foot of the page, saw the square that corresponded to the number, and read it: it said there was a person she should look for at mass on Sunday. Everyone congratulated Dona Felismina, who smiled contemptuously but was secretly hopeful.

Others threw the dice, and Rangel continued to read each one's fortune. He read in an affected, pretentious manner. From time to time he removed his glasses and cleaned them very slowly with the tip of his cambric handkerchief, either to show everyone it was cambric or because it gave off a fine scent of jasmine. Because he affected such manners, everyone called him the "Diplomat."

"Go on, Diplomat, continue."

Rangel was startled. He had forgotten to read one fortune, for he had been absorbed by the row of young ladies on the other side of the table. Was he wooing one of them? Let us start at the beginning.

He was a bachelor by virtue of circumstances, not by vocation. As a youth he had a few casual romances, but with time came the itching for greatness which had prolonged his celibacy until his forty-first year, in which we now find him. He longed for a sweetheart superior to himself and his means, and he was still waiting for her. He began to attend the dances given by a rich and celebrated lawyer for whom he copied papers and who looked after him carefully. At the dances he occupied the same inferior position he held in the office: he spent the evening wandering through the halls, observing the ballroom, watching the ladies pass by, devouring with his eyes a multitude of magnificent shoulders and delightful figures. He envied the men and imitated them. He left the dances enthusiastic and determined. If there were no dances, he went to church functions, where he could see some of the foremost young ladies of the city. This was also the case in the courtyard of the imperial palace on procession days, where he went so he could see the entrances of grandes dames and people of the court—ministers, generals, diplomats, high court judges—and he knew everything about all the people and their carriages. He returned from the festivities or processions in the same condition in which he returned from the dances—impetuous, ardent, capable of winning the laurels of fortune in a single stroke.

In terms of Petrarch's Sonnet 56, "tra la spica e la man qual muro he messo,"[1] we can say that Rangel's greatest difficulty was that a wall invariably rose up between his hand and the ear of corn he desired, and he was not a man capable of scaling walls. Everything, from the abduction of women to the destruction of cities, took place in his imagination. More than once he imagined he was Minister of State, but he grew tired of decorum and decrees. He went to the extreme of declaring himself Emperor one day, the second of December, when he returned from the parade at the Palace Square. While he held this office, he imagined a revolution in which some blood was spilled—but only a small amount—and a benevolent dictatorship in which he mediated a few minor disputes. However, on the outside all his exploits were failures. In reality, he was peaceable and discreet.

At forty he became disillusioned with his ambitions, but his basic nature remained the same, and in spite of his desire to marry, he was unable to find a suitable young lady. More than one would have accepted him with great pleasure, but he lost them all because of his extreme caution. One day he noticed Joaninha, who was about nineteen, had a pair of beautiful, quiet eyes, and was innocent of all masculine conversation. Rangel had known her since she was a child. He had carried her in his arms in the Passeio Público and when there were fireworks in the Lapa district—how could he speak to her of love? But on the other hand, his status in her house was such that a match between them could be easily arranged, and he resolved to marry either Joaninha or no one at all.

This time the wall was not so high and the ear of corn was small—it would require little effort to reach over and pull it off the stalk. Rangel had spent several months in this undertaking. He made his move only after making sure that no one could see him. If anyone was near by, he quickly pretended he wasn't trying to pick the ear of corn and walked away. When he finally did reach over, it always happened that a gust of wind made the ear sway or some small bird made the leaves rustle, and that was all it took to make him draw his hand back. Time passed by in this manner, and passion took hold of him, causing many hours of anguish, always followed by higher hopes. On Saint John's Night, he finally had his first love letter ready to deliver to Joaninha. He had already had two or three opportunities to hand it to her, but he kept delaying—the night was still young! Meanwhile, he continued to read fortunes with the solemnity of a fortuneteller.

Everyone around him was whispering, laughing, or chatting merrily. Uncle Rufino, the mischievous one in the family, walked around the table

1. "A wall always rises up between the ear of corn and the hand." The same idea is expressed in the English saying, "There's many a slip between the cup and the lip."—Trans.

with a feather, tickling the girls' ears. João Viegas was worried about a friend, Calisto, who was late in arriving. Where could Calisto be?

"Everyone out! I need to use the table, let's go into the drawing room."

It was Dona Adelaide who had returned, ready to set the table for dinner. Everyone exited, and as the clerk's daughter walked it was easy to see how charming she was. Rangel accompanied her with huge, love-stricken eyes. She went to the window for a few moments while preparations were being made for the parlor games, and he went too—it was the right time to give her the letter.

In the spacious house across the way, there was a dance. Joaninha looked out the window, and so did Rangel. They saw the couples pass by in rhythm, the ladies with their silks and laces, the gentlemen refined and elegant, some bemedaled. From time to time there was a flash of diamonds, rapid and fleeting, amid the whirl of the dance. Couples chatting, dragoons glittering, men bowing, ladies fanning themselves—all this could be seen in bits and pieces through windows that did not reveal the entire ballroom, but the rest could be imagined. He, at least, was familiar with it all and explained everything to the clerk's daughter. The demon of greatness, who had seemed to be asleep, entered and performed his tricks in Rangel's heart, and here is the trick he used in his attempt to capture Joaninha's heart:

"I know someone who would fit in very well over there," murmured Rangel.

Ingenuously, Joaninha answered: "It would be you."

Flattered, Rangel smiled and could not think of anything to say. He looked toward the lackeys and the coachmen in livery, chatting in groups in the street or leaning back on the canopies of the coaches. He began to point out which coach was which: "That one belongs to Olinda, the other is Manguarape's, and there comes another from the Lapa Street side, and it's entering Mangueira Street. It's stopping across from us. Now the footman's getting out to open the door—there, he's taking off his hat and standing up straight. The top of a bald head appears, an entire head, a man, two medals, then a finely dressed lady. They're going into the entry hall and up the carpeted stairs which are decorated at the bottom with two large vases . . ."

"Joaninha, Senhor Rangel . . ."

Those damned parlor games! Just as he was thinking of a comment regarding the couple going up the stairs, and from there he was planning to give her the letter . . . But Rangel obeyed and sat down across from the girl. Dona Adelaide, leading the game of forfeits, was collecting names:

each person was to choose the name of a flower. Of course, Uncle Rufino, always mischievous, chose the squash blossom. Rangel, who wanted to avoid the trivial, mentally compared all the flowers, and when his hostess asked him which flower he had chosen, he answered slowly and sweetly: "Marigold, my dear lady."

"What a shame Calisto's not here!" sighed the clerk.

"Did he say he was coming?"

"Yes. Yesterday he even came by the office just to tell me he would arrive late, but that I should count on his being here. He had to go to a party on Carioca Street . . ."

"Apologies for two!" shouted a voice in the corridor.

"How about that! He's here!"

João Viegas opened the door. It was Calisto, accompanied by a young man whom he introduced as "Queirós, who works at the hospital. He's not related to me, even though he looks a lot like me—if you've seen one of us, you've seen the other . . ."

Everyone laughed, for it was one of Calisto's pranks. He was as ugly as the devil, while Queirós was a handsome young man of twenty-six or twenty-seven, who had black hair and dark eyes and was singularly slim. The young ladies drew back a bit, Dona Felismina lit all the candles.

"We're playing forfeits right now, and you gentlemen may join in too," said the hostess. "Would you like to play, Senhor Queirós?"

Queirós answered affirmatively and went over to the other guests. He knew some of them and exchanged a few words with them. He told João Viegas he had wanted to meet him for a long time because of a favor his father had owed him long ago, something concerning a legal matter. João Viegas didn't remember anything, even after he was told what it was, but he enjoyed hearing the news in public, looked around at everyone, and for a few minutes was speechless with delight.

Queirós entered the game while it was in full swing. After a half hour, he had become an old friend of the family. He was extremely lively, spoke with ease, and his manners were spontaneous and natural. To everyone's delight, he possessed a vast repertory of penalties for the game of forfeits, and no one was a better leader. He went from one side to the other with liveliness and animation, arranging the groups and chatting with the young ladies with such familiarity that one would have thought they had been childhood playmates.

"Dona Joaninha, here in this chair. Dona Cesária, stand on this side. Camilo, come in from that door. No, not that way, look, you should . . ."

Stiff in his chair, Rangel was dumfounded. Where had this hurricane come from? The hurricane kept on blowing, carrying the men's hats away, mussing the girls' hair and making them giggle contentedly. Queirós here, Queirós there, Queirós everywhere. Rangel went from stupefied to mortified. The scepter was falling from his hands. He did not look at Queirós, did not laugh at what he said, and answered him dryly. Inside, he was kicking himself and telling Queirós to go to hell, calling him the contented fool who pleased everyone and made them laugh, because on evenings of merriment everyone loves a clown. But even by repeating these and other worse things, he was unable to regain his freedom of spirit. He suffered genuinely, in the most intimate depths of his pride. It was painful enough that Queirós sensed Rangel's agitation, but it was even worse that he sensed he was the cause of it.

In the same way he dreamed of pleasant things, Rangel also dreamed of vengeance. In his mind he tore Queirós apart. Then, he imagined the possibility of some disaster—a pain or anything that could remove the intruder from his presence would suffice. However, there was no pain, nothing at all . . . the devil seemed to grow more cheerful by the minute, and everyone in the room was fascinated by him. Even the habitually shy Joaninha was radiant in his presence, as were the other young ladies—all the guests seemed to be at his beck and call. Since Queirós had talked about dancing, the girls went to Uncle Rufino and asked him to play a quadrille on his flute—just one.

"I can't, one of my calluses is bothering me."

"Flute?" shouted Calisto. "Ask Queirós to play something for us, and you'll see how a flute really should be played. Go and bring the flute, Rufino. Listen to Queirós. You can't imagine how beautifully he plays!"

Queirós played *Casta Diva*. "What a ridiculous thing!" said Rangel to himself, "a piece that even the urchins whistle in the streets." He looked at Queirós in order to consider whether the stance of a flutist was that of a serious man, and he concluded that the flute was a grotesque instrument. He also looked at Joaninha and saw that like everyone else, her attention was focused on Queirós, and she was enraptured, enamored of the sounds of the music. He shuddered, not knowing why. Joaninha's expression was no different from anyone else's, but Rangel nevertheless felt something that made him dislike the intruder even more. When Queirós finished playing, Joaninha applauded less than the others, and Rangel began to wonder if it was due to her usual timidness or if something special was bothering her. It was urgent that he give her the letter.

Dinner was served. Everyone entered the dining room confusedly, and happily for Rangel, he had the good fortune of sitting across from Joaninha, whose eyes were more beautiful than ever, so aglow they seemed to have become a different pair of eyes. Rangel savored them silently and completely reconstructed the dream Queirós had so suddenly shattered. He saw himself again at her side, in the house he was going to rent, the honeymoon cottage he adorned with imaginary gold. He would win a prize in the lottery and spend it all on silks and jewels for his wife, the beautiful Joaninha—Joaninha Rangel—Dona Joaninha Rangel—Dona Joana Viegas Rangel—or Dona Joana Cândida Viegas Rangel . . . no, the Cândida couldn't be left out.

"Come on, let's have a toast, Diplomat, make one of your toasts . . ."

Rangel awoke from his dream, and the entire table repeated Uncle Rufino's reminder. Joaninha herself asked him for a toast, like the one he had made the previous year. Rangel answered that he would oblige—he would begin as soon as he finished eating that chicken wing. Movement, whispers of praise. When one girl said she had never heard Rangel speak, Dona Adelaide asked in amazement: "No? You can't imagine how well he speaks—very clearly, with well-chosen words and a charming way of . . ."

As he ate, he reminisced about shreds of ideas which helped him arrange metaphors and phrases. He finished and rose from his seat with a satisfied, smug air. They were finally coming to knock on his door. The circulation of anecdotes and the mindless pranks had ended, and they were coming to him to hear something proper and serious. He looked around and saw all eyes raised and waiting. Not all of them: Joaninha's were turned toward Queirós, and his eyes met hers with a cavalcade of promises. Rangel turned pale. The words caught in his throat, but he had to speak: everyone was waiting in silence, eager for him to begin.

Finally, he began by proposing a toast to the host and his daughter. He called her a "divine thought, transported from immortality to reality," a phrase he had used three years before, which everyone should have forgotten. He also spoke about the sanctuary of the family, the altar of friendship, and gratitude, the fruit of pure hearts. Where meaning was lacking, the phrase was more specious and resounding. In all, it was a toast of ten elegant minutes which he dispatched in five and sat down.

That wasn't all. Two or three minutes later, Queirós rose for another toast, and this time the silence was even more prompt and complete. Joaninha looked down at her lap, confused as to what he might say. Rangel shuddered.

"The illustrious friend of the family, Senhor Rangel," said Queirós, "drank to the two people who share the name of today's saint. I'll drink to the person who is the saint of all days—Dona Adelaide."

Huge applause cheered this thought, and Dona Adelaide, flattered, received congratulations from each guest. Her daughter did not stop with mere congratulations. "Mother, mother!" she exclaimed, as she stood up and embraced and kissed her three or four times—a sort of letter to be read by a certain two people.

Rangel's anger turned to disappointment, and after dinner he considered leaving. But Hope, the green-eyed demon, asked him to stay, and he stayed. Who knows? It could be a passing fancy, it would be over after tonight, it was only a Saint John's Night infatuation. After all, he, Rangel, was a respected friend of the family—all he had to do was ask for her in order to have her. And it could be that Queirós lacked the means with which to marry. What exactly did he do at the hospital? Perhaps some menial job . . . With this, he examined Queirós' clothing out of the corner of his eye, threaded his way in through the seams, scrutinized the embroidery on his shirt, squeezed the knees of his trouser legs to see how much they were worn, examined the shoes as well, and concluded that Queirós was a capricious lad who probably spent everything on himself—and marriage was a serious matter. It was also possible that he had a widowed mother or unmarried sisters to support. Rangel had no family.

"Uncle Rufino, play a quadrille."

"I can't, flute after supper causes indigestion. Let's play lotto."

Rangel declared he was unable to play because he had a headache, but Joaninha approached him and asked him to be her partner. "Half for you and half for me," she said, smiling. He also smiled and accepted. They sat down next to each other. Joaninha talked to him, laughed, raised her beautiful eyes up toward him, restlessly moving her head from side to side. Rangel felt better, and it wasn't long before he felt entirely well. He went along marking numbers at random, forgetting some of the numbers, which Joaninha pointed out to him with her finger—a nymph's finger, he said to himself. His oversights became intentional so he could see the girl's finger and hear her scold: "You're very forgetful—if you're not careful, we'll lose all our money . . ."

Rangel thought about giving her the letter under the table, but since he had not yet declared himself, she would naturally receive it with alarm, and his plans would be ruined. It would be best to tell her beforehand. He looked around the table—all heads were bent over the cards, attentively following the numbers. Then, he leaned toward the right and lowered his eyes to Joaninha's cards, as if he were checking something.

"You have two squares now," he whispered.

"Not two, I have three."

"Three, that's right, three. Listen . . ."

"And you, Senhor Rangel?"

"I have two."

"What do you mean, two? You have four."

There were four. She showed them to him, leaning over, almost brushing her ear against his lips. Afterward, she looked at him, laughing and shaking her head. "Oh, Senhor Rangel! Senhor Rangel!" Rangel listened to this with singular delight. Her voice was so sweet, her expression so friendly, that he forgot about everything, took her by the waist, and led her out to dance the eternal waltz of the chimeras. House, table, guests, everything disappeared like useless products of the imagination, leaving the two of them as the only reality, whirling through space beneath millions of stars that shone especially to light their way.

No letter, nothing at all. Toward dawn, everyone went to the window to watch the guests leave the neighboring dance. Rangel recoiled with fright. He saw Queirós and Joaninha holding hands. He tried to explain it—he was just seeing things—but it quickly happened again and again, like the waves that never cease. It was difficult for him to understand that just one night, a few hours, was enough to bring two creatures together that way, but the clear and vivid truth was evident in their manners—their eyes, words, laughter, the longing with which they said good-by to each other in the morning.

He left utterly bewildered. Just one evening, just a few hours! He arrived home late and went to bed, not to sleep, but to break down into sobs. Only when he was alone did the trappings of affectation leave him, and instead of the Diplomat he was the madman who tossed about in bed, crying out and weeping like a baby, truly miserable because of his sad autumn love. The poor devil, built of fantasies, indolence, and affectation, was in substance as miserable as Othello and suffered a more cruel fate.

Othello murders Desdemona. Our lover, in whom no one had suspected such hidden passion, served as best man for Queirós when he married Joaninha six months later.

Neither these events nor the years changed his character. When the Paraguayan War broke out, he often thought of enlisting as a recruiting officer, but he never carried out this plan. However, it is certain that he won several battles and ended up as a brigadier general.

THE COMPANION

So you think what happened to me in 1860 could be put in a book? Very well, but on the sole condition that you publish nothing until after my death. You won't have to wait long—a week at the most. I'm a doomed man.

Look, I could even tell you my whole life story—it has other points of interest—but that would take time, spirits, and paper. There's plenty of paper, but my spirits are low, and my time can be likened to the life of a nightlamp's flame. Tomorrow's sun is on its way—a relentless sun, inscrutable like life. So good-by, dear friend, read this and wish me well. Forgive whatever appears evil to you, and don't be surprised if what I have to say gives off an odor quite distinct from that of a rose. You asked me for a human document, and here it is. Don't ask for the Empire of the Great Mogul or photographs of the Maccabees, but if you request my dead man's shoes, I'll will them to you alone.

You already know it happened in 1860. About August of the preceding year, when I was forty-two years old, I became a theologian, that is to say, I copied out theological tracts for a priest in Niterói, a former classmate who thus tactfully provided me with room and board. In that same month of August 1859, he received a letter from the vicar of a village in the interior, asking if he knew someone intelligent, discreet, and patient who would be willing to go and take care of a certain Colonel Felisberto in return for a good salary. When the priest told me of the position, I jumped at the opportunity, as I had grown weary of copying Latin quotations and ecclesiastical formulas. On the way to my new job, I stopped off in Rio de Janeiro to say good-by to my brother.

When I arrived at the village, I heard more about the colonel. He was an unbearable, strange, and demanding person, and even his friends found his behavior extremely difficult to tolerate for long. He used up more companions than medicines. Two of them had had their faces bashed in. I replied that I was not afraid of healthy people, much less of a sick man. After talking with the vicar, who confirmed what I had been told and recommended gentleness and loving kindness, I proceeded to the colonel's residence.

I found him stretched out in a chair on the veranda, breathing heavily. He didn't receive me badly. At first he said nothing. Then, as he fixed his watchful cat's eyes on me, a sort of malevolent smile lit up his severe features. Finally, he said all his companions had been insolent good-for-nothings, always sleeping on the job or sniffing after the maids. Two were even thieves!

"Are you a thief?"

"No, sir."

Then he asked me my name. I told him and he looked startled. "Colombo?" "No, sir—Procópio José Gomes Valongo." He found Valongo a strange name and proposed calling me simply Procópio. I replied that whatever name suited him was fine with me. I mention this incident not only because I think it gives a good picture of him but also because my answer made an excellent impression on him. The next day he told the vicar so himself, adding that he had never had a more likable companion. The fact is, we had a regular honeymoon that lasted one week.

On the eighth day I began the life of my predecessors—a dog's life. I no longer slept. I wasn't supposed to think about anything but his needs. I had to swallow insults and laugh at them from time to time with an air of resignation and submission, for I had learned this was a way of pleasing him. His impertinence probably proceeded as much from his maladies as from his temperament, since he suffered from a whole litany of illnesses—aneurysm and rheumatism as well as three or four minor complications. He was close to sixty and had been used to having his own way since he was five. Had he only been cantankerous I might have managed, but he was malicious as well and took pleasure in the pain and humiliation of others. At the end of three months, I had tired of him and resolved to leave. All I needed was an excuse.

I didn't have to wait long. One day when I missed giving him his massage on time, he reached for his cane and dealt me two or three blows. That was the last straw. I resigned immediately and went to pack my trunk. He came to my room and asked me to stay, telling me I should forgive an old man's petulance. He kept pleading until I finally gave in.

"I'm in a tight spot, Procópio," he said one night. "I can't live much longer. Here I am, with one foot in the grave. You've got to go to my funeral, Procópio. Under no circumstances will I release you. You've got to go and pray over my grave. If you don't," he added laughing, "my ghost will come back at night and haunt you. Do you believe in spirits from the other world, Procópio?"

"Of course not!"

"And why shouldn't you believe, stupid?" he rejoined excitedly, his eyes bulging.

That's what his truces were like—imagine the wars! There were no more canings, but the insults were the same, if not worse. With time I became hardened and paid no attention to any of it. I was an ass, a dolt, an imbecile, a lazy lout—I was everything! There was no one else to serve as a target for his insults. He had no kin. A nephew from Minas Gerais had died of consumption toward the end of May or the beginning of June. His friends came by now and then to flatter him or indulge his whims, but their visits were short, ten minutes at the most. I alone was there to receive his dictionary full of names. More than once I decided to leave, but at the urging of the vicar, I stayed on. Not only was my relationship with the colonel becoming increasingly intolerable, but I was anxious to get back to Rio. At the age of forty-two, I had no intention of being strapped to a life of isolation in the backlands with a nasty old boor of a patient. To give you an idea of my seclusion, it will suffice to say that I didn't even read the newspapers. Except for occasional bits of the more important news, passed on to the colonel by his visitors, I knew nothing of the outside world. I therefore intended to return to Rio at the first opportunity, even if it meant quarreling with the vicar. Since I'm making a general confession, I should mention that having set aside all my wages, I was anxious to get back to Rio to squander them.

It was quite likely that the opportunity to leave would soon present itself. The colonel's condition had grown worse, and he had drawn up his will with the aid of a notary, who received almost as many insults as I. He was harder to cope with and his brief lapses into calm and gentle behavior became rarer. As by then I had lost the small measure of compassion that had made me excuse the old invalid's excesses, I was seething with hatred and disgust. At the beginning of August, I made a firm decision to leave. The vicar and the doctor accepted my reasons for going but asked that I stay a little while longer until a replacement could be found. I gave them a month, after which time I said I would leave no matter what the situation was.

You'll now see what happened. On the night of the twenty-fourth of August, the colonel had a fit of rage, knocked me down, called me all kinds of filthy names, threatened to shoot me, and finally threw a bowl of porridge at me, which he said was cold. The bowl hit the wall and broke into a thousand fragments.

"You'll pay for it, thief!" he screamed.

He went on grumbling for some time. About eleven he fell asleep. While he slept, I took out of my pocket an old translation of a d'Arlincourt romance I had found lying about and settled down to read in the same room, a short distance from the bed. Either because of my weariness or the book's dullness, before I reached the end of the second page I had dozed off. I awoke with a start at the sound of the colonel shouting and got up, half-asleep. He seemed to be delirious. The shouting continued, and finally he seized his water jug and hurled it at me. Before I could dodge the jug, it hit me on the left cheek, and the pain was so great I could no longer contain myself. I lunged at the old invalid and put my hands around his throat. We struggled, and I strangled him. When I realized he was no longer breathing, I stepped back in alarm and cried out, but nobody heard me. I returned to the bed and shook him to try to bring him back to life, but it was too late. The aneurysm had burst and the colonel was dead. I went into the adjacent parlor and remained there for two hours, not daring to return to his room. It would be impossible to tell you everything that went through my mind during that time. I was in a state of vacant and stupefied delirium. It seemed as though the walls had faces, and I thought I heard muted voices. The cries uttered by the victim before and during the struggle continued to reverberate inside me, and wherever I turned the air seemed to shake convulsively. Don't think for a moment that I'm just making nice images or aiming at stylistic effects. I swear that I distinctly heard voices shouting "Murderer! Murderer!" But all was quiet. The slow, measured ticking of the clock accentuated the silence and solitude. I glued my ear to the door in the hope of hearing a moan, a word, an insult, any sign of life that would have set my conscience at rest. I was even ready to let the colonel strike me at will. But I heard nothing, all was silent. I paced the room aimlessly. Then I sat down, with my head in my hands, and regretted ever having come to the place.

"Cursed be the hour in which I accepted such a position!" I cried. And I heaped abuse on the priest at Niterói, who had got me the position, and the doctor and the vicar, who had persuaded me to stay on a bit longer. I convinced myself that they were accomplices in my crime.

As the silence finally terrified me, I opened the window in the hope of finding relief in the sound of the wind. But the air was still. The night was quiet, and the stars were sparkling with the indifference of those who momentarily remove their hats for a passing funeral procession while continuing to speak of other things. I stood at the window for some time, gazing out into the night and making a mental summary of my life so I might find respite from my anguish. It was only then that I was struck by the thought of punishment. I had committed a crime and found punishment was inevitable. At this point fear was added to my feeling of remorse. I felt my hair standing on end. Minutes later I thought I saw several human forms spying on me from the grounds, where they seemed to be lying in ambush. When I stepped back they disappeared into thin air—I had suffered a hallucination.

Before daybreak I treated the wounds on my face. Only then was I able to summon up the courage to return to the dead man's room. I hesitated twice, but it had to be done, so I went in. I didn't approach the bed right away. My legs were trembling, my heart was pounding, and I even thought of running away. But that would have been the same as admitting to the murder. It was therefore urgent that I quickly efface all traces of the crime. I went up to the bed and saw the corpse with its eyes staring and its mouth open, as though it were pronouncing the question of the centuries: "Cain, what hast thou done with thy brother?" I saw my fingernail marks on his neck, so I buttoned his shirt up high and drew the top of the sheet up to his chin. Then I called a slave, told him the colonel had died in his sleep, and had him notify the vicar and the doctor. My first impulse was to leave immediately under the pretext that my brother was ill. I had in fact received a letter from him several days earlier, saying he wasn't feeling well. But I realized that a sudden departure might arouse suspicion, so I stayed. I laid out the corpse myself with the help of a near-sighted old Negro. I never left the room where the corpse was laid out, as I was afraid somebody might detect something. I wanted to be there to find out if someone suspected me, but I was afraid to look anyone in the eye. Everything irritated me: the stealthy steps with which the callers entered the room, their whisperings, the priest's ritual and prayers. When it was time to close the coffin, I did so with such trembling hands that somebody commented upon it with pity.

"Poor Procópio! Despite what he suffered he's deeply grieved."

I thought the person was being sarcastic. I was in a hurry to get it all over with. I was badly shaken when we passed from the semidarkness of the house into the street, as I feared it would be impossible to conceal the crime in full daylight. I stared at the ground and kept walking. When it was all over, I heaved a sigh of relief. I was at peace with mankind, but not with my conscience. The first few nights were naturally filled with uneasiness and distress. I don't have to tell you that I left immediately for Rio. But even there I lived in terror, though I was far from the scene of the crime. I never laughed, hardly talked, ate very little, and suffered from hallucinations and nightmares.

"Forget him, he's dead and gone," people told me. "There's no reason to be so sad."

And I took advantage of this illusion, praising the dead man highly, calling him a kind soul, difficult to be sure, but with a heart of gold. Thus singing his praises, I even convinced myself of his kindness, if only momentarily. Another matter of interest which may prove useful to you is that I, not at all religious, had a mass said at the Church of the Holy Sacrament for the eternal rest of the colonel's soul. I sent no invitations, nor did I say anything to anyone. I attended the service alone and remained on my knees the whole time, crossing myself frequently. I paid the priest double and distributed alms at the door, all in the name of the deceased. The fact that I went to the church alone should prove that I wasn't trying to deceive anyone. I might add that I never referred to the colonel without saying "May God rest his soul!" And I told some great stories about him which emphasized the pleasant and humorous aspects of his character. A week after my arrival in Rio, I received a letter from the vicar, telling me the colonel's will had been found and I was his sole heir. Imagine my amazement! I thought I was reading the letter wrong and showed it to my brother and my friends—they all confirmed what I had read. It was there in black and white. I even began to think it was a trap, but then I realized that there were other ways of catching me if the crime had been discovered. Besides, I knew the vicar was an honest man who would not have allowed himself to be used in this fashion. I reread the letter countless times—there was no doubt that I was the colonel's heir.

"How much was he worth?" my brother asked.

"I can't say for sure, but he was rich."

"Well, he's certainly proven he was your friend."

"Yes, he really was."

Thus, through an irony of fate, the colonel's possessions found their way into my hands. I considered refusing the inheritance. It seemed horrible to accept even a penny from that estate—it would make me worse than a hired assassin. I thought about this for three days but was always brought up sharp by the thought that my refusal might give rise to suspicion. Then I decided on a compromise: I would accept the inheritance and give it all away secretly, a little at a time. This idea wasn't merely a result of my scruples, it was also a way of atoning for my crime through an act of virtue. I felt this would balance the account.

I got ready and set off for the village. The closer I came to it, the more I thought about the unhappy event. The environs bore an air of tragedy, and the colonel's ghost seemed to loom at every turn in the road. My imagination kept reproducing his words, his struggle, his appearance on that horrible night of the murder . . .

But was it really murder? Actually, it was a struggle in which I had been attacked and defended myself, and in the course of my defense . . . It was a tragic struggle, an unfortunate stroke of fate. I seized upon this idea. When I balanced the offenses, the colonel's blows and insults tipped the scale in my favor. But he was not to blame for his behavior, as I well knew: his condition had made him cantankerous and even wicked . . . so I forgave him everything, everything . . . The worst was the fateful event of that night. I reflected that he couldn't have lived much longer. Even he had felt his days were numbered and had said so himself. How long would he have lived? Two weeks? One? Perhaps even less. The poor man's continual suffering wasn't life, it wasn't even a caricature of life. And who knows . . . perhaps the struggle and his natural death occurred at the same time. That was not only possible, it was even quite probable. I held fast to this idea too.

Close to the village, I panicked and wanted to turn back, but I gained control of myself and went on. Everyone congratulated me. The vicar explained the terms of the colonel's will to me, telling me of his gifts to charity, and he kept praising the Christian patience and loyalty with which I had served the colonel, who despite all his harshness and brutality had shown his gratitude in the end.

"Quite so," I said, looking away.

I was stunned. Everybody praised my devotion and patience. The immediate formalities of the inventory kept me in the village for some time. I got a lawyer and everything went along smoothly. During this time I heard much about the colonel. The villagers came and told me about him, but without the vicar's moderation and restraint. I defended him, pointed out some virtues, and said he was a bit difficult.

"Difficult, hell! He's dead and gone now, but he was the very devil!"

And they described perverse cases of cruelty and brutality, some of them quite extraordinary. At first I was merely curious regarding these instances, then I began to feel a singular pleasure which I sincerely tried to expel from my heart. I made excuses for the colonel and attributed some of their faultfinding to local rivalries. I admitted he was a little violent.

"A little? He was a raging viper!" interrupted the barber. The tax collector, the pharmacist, the notary, and everyone else agreed.

Then other stories followed, and the dead man's entire life was reviewed. The old people remembered his cruelties as a child. And my pleasure—secret, silent, and insidious—kept growing within me like a moral tapeworm which, no matter how many pieces you eliminated, immediately repaired the damage and remained more entrenched than ever.

My duties in connection with the inventory kept me occupied, and besides, public opinion in the village was so hostile to the colonel that my surroundings were beginning to lose the foreboding appearance they had held for me at first. When the inheritance finally came into my hands, I converted it into bonds and cash. Many months had passed by then, and the idea of distributing it all in alms and charitable gifts no longer had such a hold on me—I even began to think this would be sheer affectation. I made some contributions to the poor, donated some new vestments to the main church in the village, gave alms to the Sacred House of Mercy, and so on. In all, I gave away thirty-two thousand dollars, the rest I kept. I also had a marble monument raised for the colonel by a Neapolitan sculptor, who was in Rio until 1866 and then went off to die somewhere in Paraguay, if I'm not mistaken. The years have rolled by and my memory has turned dim and unreliable. Sometimes I think of the colonel, but no longer with the terror of those early days. I have told several doctors about his afflictions. All agreed his death was certain and were amazed he had lived as long as he did. I may have exaggerated a little in my description of his condition. But the truth is, he would have died anyway, even if there had been no . . . accident . . .

Good-by, dear friend. If you think these notes are worth anything, repay me with a monument in marble, and use as my epitaph this slightly emended verse from the Sermon on the Mount: "Blessed are those that have possessions, for they shall be consoled."

EVOLUTION

My name is Inácio; his, Benedito. Out of a sense of modesty I will not reveal the rest of our names, a gesture all discreet people will appreciate. Inácio will suffice. Content yourselves with Benedito. It isn't much, but it is something, and it is in keeping with Juliet's philosphy. "What's in a name?" she asked her lover. "A rose by any other name would smell as sweet." Let's go on to the scent of Benedito.

Let us first establish the fact that Benedito was the person least like Romeo in this world. He was forty-five when I met him; I won't say when, for everything in this story is to be mysterious and disjointed. He was a man of forty-five years and many black hairs—he submitted those that weren't black to a chemical process so effective that one could not distinguish the naturally black hairs from the others, except when he got out of bed in the morning, but no one ever saw him when he got out of bed. Everything else was natural—legs, arms, head, eyes, clothes, shoes, watch chain, and walking stick. Even the diamond pin he wore in his tie was natural and legitimate and had cost him a considerable sum. I myself saw him buy it at the shop that belongs to . . . there, the name of the jeweler nearly slipped out. It suffices to say the shop is on Ouvidor Street.

Morally, he was himself. No one's character changes, and Benedito's was good—or better said, peaceable. Intellectually, however, he was less original. We can compare him to a well-frequented inn where ideas from everywhere and of every kind meet and sit at the dinner table with the innkeeper's family. At times it happens that two enemies or simply two obnoxious people are there at the table, but no one argues, for the inn-keeper imposes mutual tolerance among his guests. It was in this man-ner that Benedito managed to accommodate a sort of vague atheism as well as two religious brotherhoods he founded—I don't know whether they were in the Gávea, Tijuca, or Engenho Velho district. Thus, he indiscrimi-nately wore impiety, devotion, and silk hose. Please note that I never saw his hose, but he kept no secrets from his friends.

We met on a trip to Vassouras. We had left the train and boarded the stagecoach that was to take us from the station into town. We exchanged a few words and in no time were conversing freely, at the whim of circum-stances that had imposed familiarity upon us, even though we were not yet formally acquainted.

Naturally, the first topic of our conversation was the progress the rail-roads had brought us. Benedito recalled the time when all journeys were made on the back of a donkey. We then told some anecdotes, talked about certain people, and came to agree that railroads were a necessary condition for progress in our country. Anyone who has ever traveled knows the value that one of these serious, solid banalities has in dissipat-ing the boredom of a journey. The spirit airs itself, the muscles receive a pleasant message, the blood does not shift direction, and one remains at peace with God and mankind.

"Won't our children be the ones to see this entire country crossed by railroads?"

"No, certainly not," I said. "Do you have any children?"

"None."

"Neither do I. At any rate, not even in fifty years will we see railroads throughout the entire country, but in the meantime, they are our foremost necessity. I compare Brazil to a child that is still crawling—it will only begin to walk when it has many railroads."

"What a beautiful idea!" exclaimed Benedito, with a twinkle in his eye.

"It doesn't matter to me if it's beautiful, as long as it's sound."

"Beautiful and sound," he amiably replied. "Yes, sir, you're right. Brazil is still crawling—it will only begin to walk when it has many railroads."

We arrived in Vassouras. I went to the home of the municipal judge, a longtime friend. Benedito stayed for a day and continued on to the interior. A week later, I returned to Rio alone, and a week after that, he returned. We met at the theater, chatted a great deal, and exchanged news, and Benedito ended up inviting me to have lunch with him the following day. I accepted the invitation, and he gave me a lunch fit for a king, good cigars, and lively chat. I noticed that his talk had been most effective during the middle of our trip to Vassouras, for it reduced the tedium of the journey, refreshed the spirit, and left me at peace with God and mankind, and I must say that the excellent lunch could have made me disregard the less profound moments of his conversation. It was really a magnificent meal, and it would be a historical impertinence to set Lucullus' table in Plato's house. Between the coffee and the cognac, as he rested his elbows on the table and stared at his lighted cigar, he told me: "On my last journey, I had the opportunity to see that you were right when you said Brazil is still crawling."

"Ah!"

"Yes, sir, things are exactly as you said in the stagecoach to Vassouras. We'll begin to walk only when we have many railroads. You can't imagine how true it is."

He made many observations on the customs of the interior, the backwardness and the difficulties of life there, recognizing at the same time the people's good intentions and their aspirations for progress. Unfortunately, the government was not satisfying the country's needs—it even seemed to be interested in keeping Brazil behind the other American nations. But it was indispensable that we persuade ourselves that principles are everything and men are nothing. People are not made for governments, governments are made for people, and *abyssus abyssum invocat*.[1] Then he showed me other rooms in his house, all of which had been hurriedly furnished. He showed me his collections of paintings, coins, old books, stamps, weapons. He had swords and foils, but he confessed he did not know how to fence. Among the paintings I saw a portrait of a beautiful woman. I asked him who she was. Benedito smiled.

"I won't mention it again," I said, also smiling.

"No, there's no denying it," he replied, "she was a girl I really cared for. Pretty, don't you think? You can't imagine how beautiful she was: lips of carmine, cheeks like roses, and her eyes were as dark as the night. And what teeth! Veritable pearls. A gift from nature."

Next, we proceeded to his study. It was spacious, elegant, a bit trivial, but nothing was lacking. It contained a map of the world, two maps of Brazil, and two bookcases filled with well-bound books. The desk was of finely worked ebony. On top of it, casually opened, was an almanac by Laemmert. The inkstand was made of crystal—"rock crystal," he told me, de-

1. "One abyss attracts another."—Trans.

scribing the inkstand in the same way he described the other objects. In the adjoining room there was an organ. He played the organ and enjoyed music very much, speaking of it enthusiastically, citing the best passages from certain operas. He informed me that when he was small he had begun to learn to play the flute, though he soon gave it up, which was a pity, he concluded, because it is a truly expressive instrument. He showed me yet other rooms, and then we went out into the garden, which was splendid, for art aided nature as much as nature aided art. For example, he had roses of all types and from all regions. "There's no denying," he told me, "that the rose is the queen of flowers."

I left enchanted. We ran into each other several times in the street, at the theater, and at the homes of friends we had in common, and I began to esteem him. Four months later, I went to Europe on business that obliged me to be away for a year. He remained in Brazil because of the coming election, for he wanted to be elected to the Chamber of Deputies. I was the one who had induced him to run for office, though I had done it without the least political motive. I had made the remark with the sole purpose of pleasing him and had said it in a casual way, as if complimenting him on the cut of his jacket. However, he took the idea seriously and announced his candidacy. One day, as I was crossing a Paris street, I suddenly came upon him.

"What are you doing here?!" I exclaimed.

"I lost the election," he said, "and I've come to tour Europe."

We traveled together throughout the rest of our stay in Europe. He confessed to me that losing the election hadn't discouraged him from the idea of entering Parliament. On the contrary, it had encouraged him even more. He spoke to me of his great plan.

"I want to see you elected minister," I told him.

Benedito hadn't anticipated these words. He beamed, but he hurriedly disguised his pleasure.

"I don't know about that," he answered. "However, if I do become minister, you can believe I'll only be industrial minister. We're all tired of political parties. We need to develop the potential strengths and great resources of our country. Do you remember what we said in the coach to Vassouras? Brazil is still crawling—it will only begin to walk when it has many railroads."

"You're right," I agreed, a bit startled. "Do you know why I came to Europe? I came because of a railroad. I'm making arrangements for it in London."

"Really?"

"Yes, it's true."

I showed him the papers, and he looked them over with fascination. Since I had put together some notes, statistical data, leaflets, reports, and copies of contracts referring to industrial matters, Benedito declared he was also going to collect some of these things. I actually saw him at ministries, banks, and corporations, requesting notes and pamphlets which subsequently accumulated in his luggage. However, the ardor with which he did this, though intense, was short-lived—it was only on loan. With much more enthusiasm he collected political slogans and parliamentary formulas, and he had a vast arsenal of them in his memory. In his conversations with me, he repeated them frequently, with an air of professional expertise—he found great prestige and inestimable value in them. Many of these slogans were from the British parliamentary tradition, and he preferred these over the others, as if they brought with them a bit of the House of Commons. He savored them to such an extent that I doubt that he would ever accept real liberty if he could not have his slogans along with it. I even believe that if he had had to choose between the two, he would have opted for those convenient, axiomatic, quaint, and high-sounding short formulas which do not force anyone to ponder their meaning, always fill in the gaps in conversations, and leave everyone at peace with God and mankind.

We returned to Brazil together. He went to Rio, but I remained in Pernambuco and later went back to London. I returned to Rio a year later, and by that time Benedito had been elected deputy. I went to visit him and found him preparing his maiden speech. He showed me some notes, fragments of reports, and books on political economy, some of which had pages marked with strips of paper which bore the following headings: Exchange, Land Taxes, The Cereal Problem in England, John Stuart Mill's Opinion, Thiers' Error Regarding Railroads, and so on. He was sincere, conscientious, and impassioned. He spoke to me about these things as if he had just discovered them, explaining everything *ab ovo*—he was determined to show the practical men of the Chamber that he was also practical. Then he asked me about my railroad enterprise, and I told him how it was progressing.

"I'm counting on inaugurating the first piece of track within two years."

"And what about the British investors?"

"What about them?"

"Are they satisfied?"

"Very much so. You can't imagine . . ."

I related a few technical particularities which he listened to distractedly, either because my narrative was extremely complicated or for some other reason. When I finished, he told me he was happy to see me dedicated to the industrial movement and added that he was the man the industrial movement really needed. With this in mind, he did me the favor of reading me the introduction to the speech he was to deliver in a few days.

"It's only a rough draft," he explained, "but the main ideas are here." And he began: "In the midst of the increasing spiritual unrest and the partisan uproar which conceals the voice of legitimate interests, allow someone to voice a plea from the nation. Gentlemen, it is time to consider exclusively—note that I'm saying *exclusively*—the material improvement of our country. I am not unaware of how you may answer me: you will say that a nation is composed not only of a stomach for digesting but also of a head for thinking and a heart for feeling. I answer you that all this will be worth little or nothing if it does not have legs for walking, and here I will repeat what I said to a friend a few years ago, on a trip through the interior: Brazil is a child that is still crawling—it will only begin to walk when it is crossed by railroads . . ."

I was unable to listen further and grew pensive. More than pensive, I grew astonished, bewildered in the presence of the abyss that psychology was opening at my feet. "This man is sincere," I thought, "and he believes what he wrote." I went down into the abyss to see if I could find the explanation for the channels through which that memory from the Vassouras stagecoach had passed. Forgive me if there is presumption in this, but there I found one more result of the law of evolution, as Spencer defined it—Spencer or Benedito, one of the two.

ADAM AND EVE

It was some time during the 1700s that the wife of a Bahian plantation owner, who had invited several intimate friends to dinner, announced a special kind of dessert to one of the guests, who was known to be quite a glutton. He immediately wished to know what it was, and the lady of the house called him a curious fellow. Nothing else was necessary—shortly thereafter, everyone was discussing curiosity, whether it was a masculine or a feminine trait and whether Adam or Eve was responsible for the fall from Paradise. The ladies said it was Adam's fault, and the gentlemen said it was Eve's. The judge didn't say anything and Father Bento, a Carmelite priest, replied with a smile when his hostess, Dona Leonor, asked for his opinion: "I, my dear lady, play the viola." He wasn't lying, for he was no less distinguished as a violist and harpist than as a theologian.

When the judge was called upon, he responded that there was no basis for forming an opinion, because the fall from Paradise did not occur in the way it is told in the first book of the Pentateuch, which is apocryphal. Amid the general astonishment, there was laughter from the Carmelite, who knew that the judge was one of the most pious men in the city and also that he was jovial, inventive, and even quite a joker, as long as matters remained priestly and refined. In serious matters, he was very serious.

"Father Bento," said Dona Leonor, "tell Senhor Veloso to be quiet."

"I won't tell him to be quiet," replied the priest, "because I know that everything he says is well intentioned."

"But the Scriptures . . ." said the army commander, João Barbosa.

"Let's leave the Scriptures in peace," interrupted the Carmelite. "Naturally, Senhor Veloso is acquainted with other books . . ."

"I know the authentic version of the story," insisted the judge, as he took the plate of sweets Dona Leonor offered him, "and I am ready to tell you what I know, as long as you do not ask me to do otherwise."

"Go on, please tell us!"

"This is how it really happened. In the first place, it wasn't God who created the world, it was Satan . . ."

"Good heavens!" exclaimed the ladies.

"Don't say that name," requested Dona Leonor.

"Yes, it seems that . . ." intervened Father Bento.

"Let's call him the Evil One, then. It was the Evil One who created the world, but God, who could read his thoughts, allowed him to act freely but took care to emend and polish his work, so that salvation or charity would not be left vulnerable to the forces of evil. Divine action soon appeared, because after the Evil One created darkness, God created light, and that is how the first day was created. On the second day, when the waters were created, storms and hurricanes were born, but the gentle afternoon breezes descended from divine thought. On the third day, the earth was created, and from it sprang forth the plants, but only those that bear no fruit or flowers: the thorny ones, and the deadly ones, like the hemlock. However, God created the fruit-bearing trees and the plants that nourish or are pleasing to man. Since the Evil One had hollowed out abysses and caverns in the earth, God created the sun, the moon, and the stars—such was the fourth day's work. On the fifth day, the animals of the earth, water, and air were created. We are now approaching the sixth day, and here I ask for your undivided attention."

It wasn't necessary to ask for it, for everyone was staring at him with curiosity.

Veloso continued, saying that on the sixth day Man was created, and Woman soon afterward. Both of them were beautiful, but they possessed only base instincts and lacked souls, which the Evil One could not give them. God infused souls into them with one breath, and noble, pure sentiments with another. Divine grace did not stop there—God caused a garden of delights to sprout forth and led Adam and Eve there, granting them possession of everything. Both fell at the Lord's feet, spilling forth tears of gratitude.

"You will live here," the Lord said to them, "and you may eat all fruits except the ones from this tree, which is the Tree of Knowledge of Good and Evil."

Adam and Eve listened submissively, and when they were left alone, stared at each other in amazement—it seemed that both of them had become different people. Before God granted her noble feelings, Eve had contemplated tying Adam up with a rope, and Adam had desired to beat her. Now, however, they were absorbed in contemplation of one another and the splendid natural scenery. Never before had they known air so pure, water so fresh, or flowers so beautiful and fragrant, nor did the sun spill forth such torrents of light anywhere else. Hand in hand they roamed, laughing heartily at first, because until then they had not known how to laugh. They had no conception of time, and thus their idleness did not give way to tedium—they lived in a state of contemplation. In the evenings they went to see the sun set and the moon rise and counted the stars. It was seldom that they were able to count even a thousand, for they usually fell asleep and slept like two angels.

Naturally, the Evil One became furious when he discovered all this. He couldn't go to Paradise because everything there was averse to him, nor could he bring himself to confront the Lord. Then, hearing a rustling of dry leaves on the ground, he looked down and saw a serpent. Excited by this discovery, he called to her: "Come here, snake, you creeping bile, venom of venoms, will you be your father's ambassador and reclaim his works?"

With her tail, the serpent made a vague gesture that seemed to be affirmative. The Evil One gave her the power of speech, and she answered that yes, she would go wherever he might send her—to the stars, if he would give her the wings of an eagle; to the sea, if he would reveal to her the secret of breathing under water; to the depths of the earth, if he would teach her the talents of the ant. The malign one rambled on without pause, content and extravagant with her speech, but the Evil One interrupted her: "Nothing like that, not to the air, the sea, or the depths of the earth, only to the Garden of Delights, where Adam and Eve live."

"Adam and Eve?"

"Yes, Adam and Eve."

"Two beautiful creatures we saw some time ago, walking as straight and tall as palm trees?"

"The very same ones."

"Oh, I detest them! Adam and Eve? No, no, send me somewhere else. I detest them! The mere sight of them makes me sick. You won't want me to do them any harm . . ."

"But I do!"

"Really? Then I'll go, I'll do whatever you wish, my lord and father. Now hurry and tell me what you want me to do. Bite Eve's heel? I'll bite . . ."

"No," interrupted the Evil One. "I want exactly the opposite. There is a tree in the garden, the Tree of Knowledge of Good and Evil, which they are forbidden to touch and whose fruits they are forbidden to eat. Go, coil yourself up in this tree, and when one of them passes by, call to him gently, pick up one of the fruits, and offer it to him, saying it is the most delicious fruit in the world. If he refuses, you will insist that he take it, saying that he needs only to eat it in order to learn the secret of life itself. Go, go . . ."

"I'll go, but I won't speak to Adam, I'll speak to Eve. I'll go, I'll go. Do you really mean the secret of life itself?"

"Yes, that's right. Go forth, serpent of my flesh, flower of evil, and if you are successful, I swear you'll possess the human part of creation, which is the best part, because you'll have the heels of many Eves to bite and the blood of lots of Adams in which to inject the virus of evil. Go, go, and don't forget . . ."

Forget? She already knew everything by heart. She went and entered the earthly paradise, slithered over to the Tree of Knowledge, coiled herself up, and waited. Eve appeared shortly afterward, walking gracefully and alone, with the confidence of a queen who knows no one will rob her of her crown. Torn with envy, the serpent was about to summon poison to her tongue, but she remembered she was there at the Evil One's orders and called Eve with a honeyed voice. Eve was startled.

"Who is calling me?"

"It is I, I'm eating this fruit . . ."

"You wretch! That's the Tree of Knowledge of Good and Evil!"

"That's right. I know everything now, the origin of things and the secret of life. Go on, take a bite, and you'll gain great powers on earth."

"No, you treacherous snake!"

"You fool! How can you refuse the splendor of the ages? Listen to me, do as I say, and you'll be legion, you'll found cities, and your name will be Cleopatra, Dido, Semiramis. Heroes will be born of your womb and you'll be Cornelia. You'll hear a voice from Heaven and you'll be Deborah. You'll sing and you will be Sappho. And one day, should God wish to descend to earth, He will choose your body, and your name will be Mary of Nazareth. What more could you desire? Royalty, poetry, divinity—you're giving up everything because of a foolish obedience. And that's not all. Nature will make you even more beautiful. The brilliant as well as the pale colors of the leaves, the sky, and the night will be reflected in your eyes. The night, in competition with the sun, will revel in your hair. The children of your womb will weave for you the most wonderful garments, create the finest perfumes, and the birds will give you their feathers, the earth its flowers, everything, everything, everything . . ."

Eve listened impassively. Adam arrived, listened to the serpent, and reaffirmed Eve's responses: nothing was worth the risk of losing Paradise, not knowledge, power, or any other earthly illusion. As they said this, they clasped hands and turned away from the serpent, who hurriedly exited to report back to the Evil One . . .

God, who had heard everything, said to Gabriel: "Go, My archangel, descend to the earthly paradise where Adam and Eve live, and take them to eternal bliss, which they deserve for their resistance to the Evil One's temptations."

Then the archangel, placing on his head the helmet which glittered like a thousand suns, traversed the heavens in an instant, reached Adam and Eve, and said to them: "Hail, Adam and Eve. Come with me to Paradise, which you have earned for your resistance to the Evil One's temptations."

Astonished and confused, Adam and Eve bowed their heads in obedience, and Gabriel held out his hands to them. The three ascended to the eternal abode, where hosts of singing angels awaited them.

"Come in, come in. The earth you abandoned is now left to the Evil One's creations, the ferocious and malevolent animals, the harmful and poisonous plants, the unclean air, the swamps. The creeping, vile, biting serpent will reign over the earth, and no creatures like you will ever bring a note of hope and piety to such an abomination."

And that was how Adam and Eve entered Heaven—to the sound of all its zithers, which united their notes in a hymn to the two apostates from Creation . . .

. . . His story finished, the judge handed his plate to Dona Leonor so she could give him more dessert, while the other guests stared at one another in amazement—instead of an explanation, they had heard a puzzling narration, or at least a story without apparent meaning. Dona Leonor was the first to speak: "I was right when I said Senhor Veloso was fooling us. He didn't do what we asked him to do, and it didn't happen the way he said it did. Isn't that right, Father Bento?"

"The honorable judge will know the answer to that," replied the Carmelite, smiling.

And as the judge lifted a spoonful of dessert to his mouth, he said: "On second thought, I don't think any of it actually occurred, but, Dona Leonor, if it had, we wouldn't be here enjoying this dessert, which is in all sincerity perfectly delicious! Is it the work of your old pastry cook from Itapagipe?"

ETERNAL!

"You don't have to tell me," I said as I entered his room. "I'll bet you're upset because of the Baroness."

Norberto wiped the tears from his eyes and sat down on his bed. I lectured him as I sat astride a chair, resting my chin on the back of it.

"How many times have I told you you're making a fool of yourself? When are you going to put an end to this ridiculous and humiliating affair? She doesn't care a whit for you and besides, don't you think it's risky? You'll see if it isn't when the Baron begins to suspect you're chasing after his wife. You'd better be careful because he looks like he has a mean temper."

In despair, Norberto clutched his head with his hands. Earlier I had received a message from him asking me to come console and advise him. He had waited for me outside my boardinghouse until one o'clock in the morning. In his letter, he said he had been unable to sleep because he'd received some terrible news, and he spoke of taking his life. Despite the fact that I had also received some bad news, I went to the aid of my poor friend. We were the same age and were both studying medicine, except that I was repeating the third year, which I had failed out of laziness. Norberto lived at home with his parents. I was not so fortunate, for my parents had died, and I lived on a monthly allowance sent by a kind old uncle from Bahia, who also paid my debts twice a year. After paying them he would immediately send me a nasty letter, but he always ended it by saying I should continue my studies at least until I had my medical degree. "Why should I take a degree?" I would ask myself. My companions were the sun, the moon, women, and fine Vilegas cigars, and none of them had taken degrees. So I laughed, frittered away my time, and allowed both the weeks and my creditors to pass by unnoticed.

I spoke of bad news. It came in the form of a letter from my uncle, which had arrived along with Norberto's. I opened my uncle's letter first and read it aghast. Addressing me formally for the first time, he said, "Sr. Simeão Antônio de Barros: I'm sick and tired of wasting my money on you. If you wish to conclude your studies, you'll have to enroll at the university in Bahia and live in my home. If you don't accept my conditions, you'll have to fend for yourself, because I'm not sending you another cent." Crumpling the letter, I fixed my eyes on an extremely cheap lithograph of the Viscount of Sepetiba, which had been hanging on the wall of my boardinghouse room ever since I had lived there. I called the portrait the ugliest names I could think of, and shouting at the top of my voice, I told my uncle he could keep his money, that my youthful desires were more important than adherence to the demands of relatives or social conventions.

Imagination, the mother of invention, soon showed me endless sources of income, which would allow me to do without the stingy old man's handful of worthless coppers. But after my initial reaction, I reread my uncle's letter and understood that standing on my own two feet would in fact be more arduous than I had initially believed. I could probably have found a good steady job and made it on my own. But I had grown so accustomed to going to Quitanda Street to pick up my monthly allowance and spending double the amount I received that it would have been difficult to get used to another arrangement.

That's when I read Norberto's letter and rushed off to his house. After my first words, he gave me a gloomy look and told me he had expected better advice from me.

"What did you want me to say?"

He didn't answer.

"Should I have told you to buy a pistol or a crowbar? Drugs, maybe?"

"Why are you making fun of me?"

"To make a man out of you."

Shrugging his shoulders and looking at me scornfully, Norberto asked me what I meant. Wasn't falling in love with the most divine creature in the world and dying because of her a sign of manliness?

The Baroness of Magalhães, the cause of Norberto's madness, was visiting Rio with her husband. Before receiving his title, which he had purchased to satisfy his wife, the Baron was known as Antônio José Soares de Magalhães. They were newlyweds when they arrived in Rio. The Baroness, an extremely beautiful woman of twenty-four, was thirty years younger than her spouse. Among family and friends she was called Iaiá Lindinha. From the moment of his arrival in Rio, the Baron and Norberto's father were in close contact with one another, as they were old friends.

"So you would die because of her?" I asked.

He swore that he was capable of taking his life. What an intriguing woman! The sound of her voice had cast a spell on him. Then he rolled over and buried his head in a pillow to smother his anguished cries and sobs and prevent those on the first floor from hearing him.

As I had grown accustomed to my friend's tears since the Baroness' arrival, I waited for him to calm down. But he didn't. I got off my chair, told him he was behaving like a child, and said good-by. He grabbed my arm to keep me from leaving and told me he had not yet come to the heart of the matter.

"Go on, finish."

"They're leaving. We were at their home yesterday, and I learned they're departing on Saturday."

"For Bahia?"

"Yes."

"Then they'll be going there with me."

I told him about my uncle's letter and the fact that he had ordered me to enroll in the medical school in Bahia and live in his home. Norberto became excited. Bahia? We could go together! We were close friends and his parents would honor our friendship. I confess that I found his plan excellent, so we did our best to convince his parents. Although his mother wept at the thought of being separated from her son, she gave in faster than we had expected. But his father was unyielding, despite our persistent entreaties. I brought the Baron specifically to help us plead our case, but not even an old friend could persuade Norberto's father to release his son, though he promised to lodge him in his own house and keep an eye on him.

You can imagine my friend's despair. Under the pretext of wanting to be with me my last night in Rio, he left his parents, came to my house, and wept harder than I've ever seen anyone weep. I couldn't deny the sincerity of his feelings nor could I presume to console him, as it was the first time he had truly fallen in love. Until then neither of us had ever received anything but cheap tokens of love. To his misfortune, the first time he received a solid coin it was made of neither gold nor silver but Lycurgus' hard steel, forged in sour vinegar.

That night we didn't sleep. Norberto wept, tore at his hair, and contrived absurd or terrible plans to solve his dilemma, speaking again of suicide. As I packed my suitcases, I attempted to console him, which only made matters worse, because it was like telling a drowning man to swim. I suggested he smoke a couple of cigarettes to help calm himself: he ended up smoking them by the dozens without finishing any. At three o'clock he proposed fleeing Rio, not right away, but on the first northbound ship, which was to depart in a few days. I got him to abandon the idea, telling him it was for his own good.

"I would agree if I were certain things would work out for you as you wish. But if you're not positive you'd be welcome you could meet with closed doors and she could send you packing."

"How can you be sure?"

"Are you *certain* she would welcome you? Is she really fond of you?"

"I can't say for sure that she is."

He told me how she had treated him and different things she had said or done, but it all seemed insignificant or inconclusive. As he wept in silence or cried out in anguish, I began to share his pain and to suffer along with him. My reason gave way to compassion and our souls were fused into one throbbing heartache. That's when I made him the following promise:

"I have an idea. I'm already acquainted with the Baron's wife, and we'll be traveling north on the same ship. I'll probably frequent their house in Bahia, and I can try to determine how she feels about you. If I see that you're not really on her mind, I'll tell you not to come, but if I detect the slightest leaning in your direction I'll let you know, and for better or worse you can embark for Bahia."

Seeing a glimmer of hope in my proposal, Norberto accepted it with a tremor of excitement. He made me swear that I would keep my promise and that I would scrutinize her carefully, saying that he, for his part, would not hesitate for an instant if I sent him favorable news. He insisted I mustn't miss a thing, claiming that the smallest clues were invaluable and that the most insignificant words could be more revealing than entire books. If the occasion presented itself, I was to allude to his state of despair. To assure unfailing commitment on my part, he said he would take his life if my mission were unsuccessful, because his love, as it was eternal, could only be requited through death and oblivion. I didn't have the heart to tell him he was obliging me to send him good news or no news at all. At the time I could only weep along with him.

Dawn was witness to our immoral pact. I didn't allow him to come aboard when we parted company. I'd prefer not talking about the trip. Oh epic seas of Homer, whipped to a froth by Eurus, Boreas, and violent Zephyr—you may toss Ulysses about but don't make him seasick! The seas we crossed between Rio and Bahia were particularly unkind to me, and I didn't dare appear before the magnificent Baroness until we were approaching Salvador. When I finally saw her, she looked fresh and poised, as though she had just taken a pleasant stroll.

"Don't you miss Rio?" I asked her, to break the ice.

"Of course I do."

The Baron named the points of interest we saw from the deck of the ocean liner and indicated the location of places we couldn't see. He also invited me to visit their home in Bonfim whenever I could. When we arrived in Bahia, my uncle came aboard, and I detected a kindly soul beneath his serious demeanor. He looked at me, the only child of his deceased sister, and saw I was obedient. I couldn't have made a better first impression. Divine youth! I was being handsomely rewarded in spite of my despicable conduct in Rio.

I spent my first days getting to know the city of Salvador. But it wasn't long before I received a letter from Norberto calling my attention to his plight. I went to Bonfim. The Baroness—or Iaiá Lindinha, which was the name everyone still used when they addressed her—and her husband gave me such a warm and hospitable reception that I became ashamed of the mission that had brought me to their home. But my shame didn't last long when I thought of my friend's despair. The need to either console or undeceive him was foremost in my mind. I even confess to a peculiar change of heart at the time: now that Norberto and the Baroness were separated, I found myself hoping she did care for him—even though I had expressed my doubts concerning her feelings for him and convinced him to stay behind until I had determined just how he stood with her. Perhaps I wanted to see him happy, or it could have been that I was confident I would win her over for the unfortunate fellow.

Naturally we talked about Rio. I told her I was homesick for the things I had taken for granted: the streets that had become part of me, familiar faces, places I used to visit, and good friends, the closest tie of all. Norberto's parents, for example, were good friends.

"Two saints," interrupted the girl. "My husband tells me some curious things about Norberto's father, whom he has known for years. Did you know that his marriage resulted from a passionate love?"

"It stands to reason. Their son is living proof of that love. Were you well acquainted with Norberto?"

"I was. He used to visit us quite often."

"You didn't *really* know him."

Iaiá Lindinha frowned slightly.

"Pardon me if I seem to contradict you," I said spiritedly. "You didn't know the kindest, purest, most passionate soul God ever created. Perhaps you think I'm biased because he's a friend. To tell the truth, he's the main reason for my being so attached to Rio. Poor Norberto! I can't think of another person cut out for two roles at the same time. I can see him as an archangel, telling us about the delights of heaven, and also as a hero, scaling the walls of heaven to reveal mankind's sorrows."

Only after speaking did I realize that what I had said was ridiculous. Iaiá Lindinha limited herself to saying that my friendship seemed very enthusiastic and that she thought my friend was a good person. She said it seemed he was unhappy or was perhaps given to periods of depression. She had been told he was very studious.

"Yes, he is."

I stopped talking about Norberto in order to avoid precipitating matters. I hope you won't condemn me for my actions before I have a chance to explain myself. I know that my role in this matter wasn't commendable, but the whole incident took place twenty-seven years ago. I have faith in Time, the illustrious alchemist. Give Father Time a handful of mud, and he'll transform it into diamonds—or gravel, at the very least. When a statesman is so unscrupulous in the writing and publication of his memoirs that he withholds nothing—neither things said in confidence, nor secrets of state, nor extremely personal details pertaining to love affairs—he'll see what a scandal the book causes. People will rightfully say that the man is a cynic, unworthy of the trust and love bestowed on him. The outcry will be sincere and legitimate because a public office imposes many restraints on its incumbent. Good manners and respect for the women he has loved constrain a statesman to silence.

But after a century has passed, the same book will become a valuable historical and psychological document. With cool objectivity readers will study the intimate life of our times: how we loved, how governmental cabinets were formed or dissolved, if women were open or dissimulating, how we held elections and courted women, if we wore shawls or capes, what kind of carriages were in vogue, if watches were worn to the right or the left, and a multitude of other interesting things relating to our society and affairs of state. Hence, my hope that my readers don't condemn me before hearing my appeal. Besides, twenty-seven years have now gone by!

I spent more than half a year knocking on the door of the Baroness' heart to see if I could find any sign of Norberto in it, but no one answered, not even her husband. If most of the letters I sent Norberto didn't hold out hope, they weren't disappointing either. Any hint of hope in the letters was a result of my own vanity and Norberto's love for her, which joined forces to pique her curiosity with the possibility of a remote intriguing mystery.

By then our relationship was close. I visited them frequently. When I didn't go there three nights in a row, I became anxious and restless. I would rush to see them on the fourth night, but it was she who awaited me at the gate of their country home to tell me I was ungrateful, lazy, and forgetful. But even though she called me names she would still wait for me outside, greeting me with outstretched hands which seemed to tremble on occasion, or perhaps my hands were the ones that trembled—I can't remember for sure. When we parted company, I would occasionally tell her in a hushed voice that I couldn't come the following day because I had to study or do something for my uncle. Although she never tried to talk me out of any previous commitments, she would nonetheless become disconsolate.

My letters to Norberto became less frequent and I scarcely mentioned laiá Lindinha's name, as though I had stopped frequenting her house. Two of the many formulas I used were "Yesterday I ran into the Baron in the Palace Square. He told me his wife is in good health," or "Can you guess who I saw at the theater three days ago? The Baroness." Since I didn't want to remind myself of my hypocrisy, I never reread my letters. For his part, Norberto wrote less and his letters were brief. The Baroness and I stopped mentioning his name, and between us it was tacitly understood that he was a corpse—a sad body that had been dispatched without a burial service.

Although the idea might seem incongruous to those who have never been in love, we began to insist that the abyss we hovered over was a reflection of the celestial dome. Death resolved our dilemma by carrying the Baron off with a stroke on March 23, 1861, at 6:00 P.M. He was an excellent man whose widow repaid him in prayers what she hadn't given him in love. Three months later, when I asked laiá Lindinha to marry me after she was out of mourning, she was neither surprised nor insulted by my request. On the contrary, she said she would marry me, but with the condition that I first finish my studies and graduate. I did my best to change her mind, but she wouldn't budge, claiming that my uncle feared I would be delayed in starting my career if I married before finishing my degree.

"And he's right," she concluded. "Listen, I'll only marry a doctor."

For some time she and a sister-in-law were chaperoned by the latter's husband on a trip through Europe. My longing to be with her was a heavier burden to bear than my classes. I abandoned my former idle ways, studied diligently, and received my graduation cape the evening before we were married. In all sincerity, I can say that I found the priest's Latin superior to the valedictory speech.

Weeks later Iaiá Lindinha proposed a trip to Rio. I agreed, but I confess that I was somewhat troubled by the thought of it. If Norberto still lived there, I would run into him. We hadn't written one another for three years, and even before that our correspondence had been brief and uninteresting. Would he know about our marriage or the events that had led up to it? We went to Rio and I kept my preoccupations to myself.

I saw no reason why I should tell my wife about my secret betrayal. After our arrival, I wondered whether I should wait for Norberto to call on me or seek him out first. I chose the second alternative so I could tell him what had happened before he discovered it on his own. I fabricated curious and unusual circumstances that had been designed by the mysterious workings of providence. Please don't laugh at me—the truth is my imagination contrived these plans with the utmost seriousness.

Within four days, I learned that Norberto was living in the vicinity of Rio Comprido. He was married, which was so much the better. I rushed off to his house. In the garden I saw a black wet nurse suckling a baby. Another child of approximately a year and a half was squatting on the ground gathering pebbles.

"Bertinho, go tell your mama there's a young man here looking for your father."

The child obeyed, but before he returned my old friend Norberto had come outside. I recognized him at once despite his bushy sideburns, and we embraced one another.

"You here in Rio? When did you arrive?"

"Yesterday."

"You've put on some weight—it becomes you. You look better than ever. Let's go in. And what can I do for you?" he said to Bertinho, who was hugging one of his legs. He leaned over to pick him up, raised him in the air, and showered him with kisses. Then, cradling him in his arms, he pointed at me.

"Do you know this gentleman?"

Not knowing what to say, Bertinho stared at us with his finger in his mouth. Norberto told him that I had been daddy's close friend when grandma and grandpa were still living.

"Your parents died?"

Giving a nod of assent, Norberto attended to his son, who was pulling at his face and asking him for more kisses. Then he went over to the wet nurse who was suckling the baby girl. He looked at his daughter with admiration as he called her endearing names and told me to come and see her. Enraptured, he saw something of himself reflected in the child. He said she was only five months old, but if I returned in fifteen years I would see a beautiful young lady. What lovely arms and chubby fingers! Unable to contain his delight, he bent over to kiss her.

"Come in and meet my wife. You'll dine with us."

"I'm already committed to dine elsewhere."

"Mommy's peeking at us," said Bertinho.

I looked and saw a young lady standing in the doorway of the living room, which led to the garden. We walked up five steps and entered. Norberto took hold of her hands and kissed them. Blushing deeply, she tried to pull them back.

"Don't be embarrassed, Carmela," he said. "This is Simeão Barros, the classmate I've talked about so often—he was an honest-to-God friend! By the way," he said, turning to me, "why didn't you answer our wedding invitation?"

"I didn't receive one," I replied.

"Well, I'm sure it was mailed."

Carmela listened to her husband admiringly. She pleased him so much that he went and sat next to her so he could hold her hand on the sly. Pretending to notice nothing, I talked about school days, friends, politics, the war, and anything else I could think of in order to avoid allowing him the opportunity to ask me if I were married. By then I was sorry I had come. What would I tell him if he asked me about Iaiá Lindinha? He said nothing, perhaps he knew nothing.

Our conversation continued until I stood up, saying I had to leave. Carmela bade me a most gracious farewell. She was beautiful, and her eyes were resplendently virtuous. It was obvious that Norberto adored her.

"Did you get a good look at her?" he said at the doorway to the garden. "There are no words to describe the strength of the bonds that hold us together. What are you smiling about? You probably find my behavior childish, and I would have to agree. I'm an eternal child, just as my love is eternal."

I climbed into a cab, promising I would return soon to dine with them.

"Eternal!" I said to myself. "Just like his love for my wife."

Turning to the coachman, I asked him, "What's eternal?"

"Pardon my saying so, sir, but I think my neighborhood tax collector is eternal. He's a real scoundrel, and if I don't punch him in the face one of these days I deserve to go to hell. The rascal's always coming around asking for money, and he has a lot of buddies who protect him. Some say he even—well, that's none of my business. But he oughta be punched in the face . . ."

I didn't hear the rest of the coachman's answer, as I was pondering the meaning of "eternal" while he droned on. When I awoke from my thoughts, we were on Glory Street, and he was still talking. I paid him and walked down past Glory and Russell beaches until I reached Flamingo Beach, where the surf was pounding heavily. The question I had asked the coachman echoed in my mind like a musical refrain: "What's eternal?" The breakers, more discreet than the coachman, didn't talk nonsense. They just kept flowing in and out, back and forth, rising and dying.

I arrived at the Hotel de Estrangeiros late in the afternoon. My wife was expecting me for dinner. When I entered the room, I took her by the hands and asked her: "Iaiá Lindinha—what's eternal?"

"How ungrateful you are! My love for you, of course!"

I dined without remorse. Quite the contrary: I was cheerful and comforted. But that's Father Time for you! Give him a handful of mud and he'll reimburse you with gems . . .

A CELEBRITY

"Oh, so you're Pestana?" asked Miss Mota, with a sweeping gesture of admiration. And immediately correcting her familiar address: "Pardon my manners, but . . . are you really he?"

Annoyed and dispirited, Pestana answered yes, it was he. He had just come from the piano, wiping his forehead with a handkerchief, and was approaching the window when the young lady made him stop. It wasn't a dance, just an intimate evening party with some twenty people, who had come to dine with the widow Camargo from Beach Street on her birthday, the fifth of November 1875. The kind and gay widow! She loved laughter and merrymaking, despite her sixty years, and this was the last time she laughed and made merry, because she passed away in the early days of 1876. The kind and gay widow! With what heart and soul she organized a dance immediately after dinner, asking Pestana to play a quadrille! She didn't even have to complete her request—Pestana bowed politely and hastened to the piano. After the quadrille, they had scarcely rested for ten minutes, when the widow darted over to Pestana again to ask for a very special favor.

"Whatever you say, madame."

"Could you play your polka *Don't Kid Me Honey* for us now?"

Pestana made a face, which he quickly concealed, bowed in silence without his customary politeness, and went to the piano without enthusiasm. After the first measures were heard a new happiness spread about the room. The gentlemen hurried to the ladies, and the pairs began to move to the tune of the latest polka. The very latest—published just three weeks earlier, there was no longer a nook or a cranny of the city, however remote, where it wasn't known. The tune was on everybody's lips.

Miss Mota was the last to suspect that the Pestana she had seen at the dinner table and then at the piano, the man dressed in a snuff-colored frock coat, with long, curly black hair, circumspect eyes, and a beardless chin, was *the* Pestana, the famous composer of polkas—her friend told her so when she saw him coming from the piano, after the polka. Hence, the admiring question. We have seen that he answered her in an annoyed and dispirited fashion. Nonetheless, the two young ladies were so unsparing in their profusion of flattering remarks that the most modestly vain person would have been pleased to hear them. Pestana received them with growing displeasure until claiming he had a headache, he finally asked permission to take his leave. No one, not even the lady of the house, succeeded in convincing him to stay. They offered him home remedies, some rest, but he accepted nothing, insisted on leaving, and left.

Once in the streets he walked quickly, for fear they might still call him back. He didn't slacken his pace until he turned the corner of Formosa Street. But even there, in that very spot, his famous and lively polka was waiting for him. Notes from his most recent hit, played on a clarinet, fluttered forth from a modest house on the right, just a few yards away. People were dancing. Pestana stopped for a moment, considered retracing his steps, but decided to go ahead. He quickened his steps and crossed to the other side of the street. The notes were finally lost in the distance, and Pestana entered Aterrado Street, where he lived. When he was almost home, he saw two men approaching him. One of them, as he was passing, began to whistle the same polka with spirit and vigor. The other caught the tempo of the music, and the two of them went down the street, boisterous and cheerful, while the composer, in desperation, ran into his house.

At home he heaved a sigh of relief. Old home, old staircase, and his old Negro servant, who came to see if he wanted to dine.

"I don't want anything," shouted Pestana. "Make me some coffee and go to bed."

He undressed, put on a nightshirt, and went to a spacious room at the back of the house. When the Negro lit the gas lamp, Pestana smiled and silently paid his compliments to the ten portraits hanging on the wall. Just one was an oil painting, of the priest who had educated him, taught him Latin and music, and who, according to idle tongues, was Pestana's own father. It is a fact that he had bequeathed that old house to him, along with the furniture, which dated back to the time of Pedro I. The priest had composed some motets and was crazy about music, sacred or profane. These tastes were instilled in the youth, or if wagging tongues are to be given some credence, they were transmitted to him through blood ties. But this is quite beside the point of my story, as you will see.

The other portraits were of classical composers: Cimarosa, Mozart, Beethoven, Gluck, Bach, Schumann, and three others. Some were engravings and others lithographs. They were of different sizes and were poorly framed, but they were positioned like saints in a church. The piano was the altar, and the evening's gospel was open there: it was a Beethoven sonata.

The coffee arrived. Pestana swallowed the first cup and seated himself at the piano. He looked at Beethoven's portrait, and losing consciousness of himself, he began to play the sonata in a distracted or absorbed manner, but with great perfection. He repeated the piece. Then he stopped for a few moments, got up, and went to one of the windows. He returned to the piano. It was Mozart's turn, so he picked up a sheet of music and executed it in the same way, with his heart somewhere else. Then Haydn kept him occupied until midnight and the second cup of coffee.

Between midnight and one o'clock, Pestana did little more than look at the portraits and stand at the window staring at the stars. From time to time he went to the piano and, standing, struck a few disconnected chords on the keyboard, as though searching for some thought, but the thought didn't come, and he resumed his position at the window. To him the stars seemed like so many musical notes affixed to the sky, just waiting for somebody to unfasten them. Someday the sky would be emptied, but by then the earth would be a constellation of musical scores. No image, thought, or moment of reflection carried any recollection of Miss Mota, who meanwhile, at that very moment, slept dreaming about him, the famous author of so many beloved polkas. The thought of marriage made the young lady lose a few minutes of sleep. And why not? She was about twenty years old, and he was thirty at most. She slept to the tune of the polka, which she knew by heart, while its author was thinking of neither the polka nor the girl but of the old classical works. He questioned the heavens and the night, begging the angels and the devil himself. Why couldn't he compose just one such immortal page?

At times it seemed as though the seed of an idea were on the verge of sprouting from the depths of his subconscious. He ran to the piano in order to give it life, to translate it into sounds, but to no avail: the idea vanished. At other times, seated at the piano, he allowed his fingers to wander at random, to see if fantasias would issue from them, as they did from Mozart's, but nothing, absolutely nothing, the inspiration didn't come and his imagination remained dormant. If by chance an idea did appear, crystal clear and beautiful, he would discover it was but an echo from another's piece, repeated in his memory. Then, irritated, he would get up, swearing that he would abandon music and go plant coffee or push a vendor's cart, but ten minutes later he was back again, with his eyes on Mozart's portrait, imitating him at the piano.

Two, three, four o'clock. After four he went to bed—he was tired, discouraged, and emotionally exhausted, and he had to teach the following day. He slept poorly, awakened at seven, got dressed, and ate breakfast.

"Would you like your cane or your umbrella?" asked the Negro, following the instructions of his master, who was so frequently distracted.

"My cane."

"But it looks like rain today."

"Rain," repeated Pestana mechanically.

"It does look like it, sir, the sky's quite dark."

Pestana stared at the Negro with uncertainty and concern. Suddenly he blurted: "Wait right there!"

He ran to the portrait room, opened the piano, sat down, and spread his fingers over the keyboard. He began to play something that was his very own, with genuine inspiration: a polka, a frolicsome polka, in the language of the billboards. No resistance on the part of the composer. His fingers drew the notes forth with ease, joining them, juggling them—it could be said that his Muse composed and danced simultaneously. Pestana forgot his pupils, forgot the Negro waiting for him with his cane and umbrella, even forgot the portraits that hung with dignity on the wall. He just composed, striking the keys or writing, without the fruitless efforts of the evening before, without irritation, without asking for the heavens' favors, without interrogating Mozart's eyes. No weariness. Life, charm, and novelty gushed forth from his heart, as from an inexhaustible spring.

Soon the polka was finished. He did correct a number of minor points when he returned for dinner, but he was already humming it in the streets, on his way home. He liked it. The blood of his paternity and his true vocation circulated in the recent, unpublished composition. Two days later, he took it to the publisher of his other polkas, which already numbered some thirty pieces. His publisher thought it was "cute."

"It's going to be a big success."

The matter of a title was brought up. In 1871, when Pestana composed his first polka, he had wanted to give it a poetic title and chose *Sundrops*. The publisher shook his head, telling him that titles had to be designed with their future popularity in mind and selected for their allusion to some important event or for the catchy effect of their words. He had two ideas: *The Law of September 28* and *Sweethearts Aren't for Fondling*.

"But what's the meaning of *Sweethearts Aren't for Fondling*?" asked the author.

"It doesn't mean anything, but it'll become popular right away."

Pestana, still unsophisticated and unpublished, refused both names and kept his polka, but it wasn't long before he had composed another, and his itch for publicity led him to publish both of them, with whatever titles seemed most attractive or appropriate to the publisher. From then on this was the procedure.

Now, when Pestana delivered his latest polka and they came to the matter of the title, his publisher said that for days he had had one in mind and had saved it for the first work he should hand over. The title was gaudy, long, and meandering: *Please Keep Your Basket to Yourself, Ma'am*.

"And for the next time," he added, "I've already got another in mind."

The first edition sold out as soon as it was put on display. The composer's fame guaranteed its popularity, but the work itself was original and in keeping with pieces done in that style: it was an invitation to dance, and it was easily memorized. Within a week it was a hit. For a time Pestana was truly in love with the piece and liked to hum it under his breath. He lingered in the street when he heard it being played in somebody's home and became angry when it wasn't played well. It was played immediately by bands in the theaters, and Pestana went to one of them to hear it. Nor was he displeased when he heard it whistled by an indistinct shape going down Aterrado Street one evening.

That honeymoon lasted only a week. Like other times, and even more on this occasion, the sight of the old masters in the portraits made him bleed with remorse. Angry and offended, Pestana turned against the one who had come to console him so many times, the Muse with mischievous eyes and rounded form, easygoing and uncomplicated. At that point his self-disgust and hatred for whoever asked him for his latest polka returned, and he resumed his efforts to compose something with a classical flavor, even if it were only a page, just one, but of a quality that would allow it to stand beside the works of Bach and Schumann. Futile study, useless effort. He plunged into that Jordan and walked away unbaptized. Thus he spent day and night, confident and stubborn, certain that his desire would bring success and that as long as he gave up light music . . .

"To hell with the polkas—the devil can dance to them!" he said one morning at daybreak, when he went to bed. But the polkas refused to go that far. They went to Pestana's house, into the portrait room itself, and burst forth in such abundance that he scarcely had time to compose them, then print them, enjoy them a few days, detest them, and return to the classical sources, which produced nothing. He lived torn between these alternatives, until and after his marriage.

"Whom is he going to marry?" Miss Mota asked her uncle, the court clerk who had given her the news.

"He's marrying a widow."

"Is she old?"

"Twenty-seven."

"Pretty?"

"No, but she's not homely either—so-so. I heard that he fell in love with her because he heard her sing in the last festival of Saint Francis of Paula. But I also heard that she possesses another gift, neither unusual or valuable: she has tuberculosis."

Court clerks aren't supposed to be spirited—ill-spirited, that is to say. In the end his niece felt a drop of balsam, which cured her little sting of envy. It was all true. A few days later, Pestana married a twenty-seven-year-old widow, who was a good singer and had tuberculosis. She would be the spiritual wife of his creative genius. Celibacy was doubtlessly the cause of his sterility and waywardness, he said to himself. Artistically he considered himself a playboy of the wee hours—his polkas were just the adventures of an idler. Yes, now he would beget a family of serious works, profound, inspired, and carefully wrought.

That hope budded in the early hours of his love and blossomed forth on the eve of his wedding. "Maria," stammered his heart, "give me what I couldn't find in the loneliness of my nights and the turmoil of my days."

In order to commemorate their marriage, he immediately took it into his head to compose a nocturne. He would call it *Ave Maria*. It was as though his happiness had brought him the dawning of an inspiration. Not wanting to say anything to his wife before it was ready, he worked in secret. This was difficult because Maria, who loved music as much as he, came to play with him, or just to listen to him play, in the portrait room for hours on end. They even held some weekly concerts with three musicians who were Pestana's friends. One Sunday, however, he could no longer hold back, and he called his wife to hear him play a passage of the nocturne. He didn't tell her what it was or who had composed it. He stopped suddenly and looked at her questioningly.

"Don't stop," said Maria, "it's Chopin, isn't it?"

Pestana became pale, stared out into space, repeated one or two passages, and got up. Maria sat down at the piano and after making an effort to recall it to her memory, executed the piece by Chopin. The idea, the motif were the same: Pestana had found them in one of those dark alleys of his memory, that old city of betrayals. Sad, desperate, he left home and went in the direction of the bridge, on the way to Saint Christopher's.

"Why fight it?" he said. "I'll stick with the polkas . . . Three cheers for the polka!"

The men who passed him and heard this stared at him as if he were a madman. And he walked along, delirious, mortified, tossed to and fro between his ambition and his vocation, in an endless game of shuttlecock. He passed the old slaughterhouse. When he reached the crossing gate of the railroad, he considered walking up the tracks until the first train came and squashed him. The guard made him move back. He came to his senses and returned home.

A few days later—at six o'clock—on a clear and fresh morning in May 1876, Pestana felt a familiar tingling in his fingers. He got up very slowly, so as not to awaken Maria, who had coughed all night and was now sound asleep. He went to the portrait room, opened the piano, and playing as quietly as he could, drew forth a polka. He had it published under a pseudonym. In the following two months he composed and published two more. Maria was not aware of anything: she just went along coughing and dying until, one evening, she expired in the arms of her terrified and desperate husband.

It was Christmas Eve. Pestana's grief was multiplied, because in the neighborhood there was a dance where a number of his best polkas were being played. At this point it was hard for him to tolerate the dance: his tunes gave him an impression of irony and perversity. He felt the rhythm of the dance steps, divined the possibly lustful movements motivated by one or another of his arrangements, and all this while he stood by the corpse of his wife, a bundle of bones stretched out on the bed. Thus all the hours of the night passed, the slow as well as the fast, dressed in tears, sweat, and cologne, dancing about endlessly, as to the tune of a polka by an immense, invisible Pestana.

After his wife was buried, the widower had one final musical goal in mind: to compose a *Requiem*, which he would have played on the first anniversary of Maria's death, after which he would abandon music. Then he would choose another line of work: clerk, mailman, street vendor, anything to make him forget Art's murderous heart and deaf ear.

He began to work on his opus, using everything at his disposal: daring, patience, meditation, even the whims of Lady Luck, whom he had used on another occasion while imitating Mozart. He reread and studied this composer's *Requiem*. Weeks and months passed. The work, which got off to a fast start, slackened its pace. Pestana had his ups and downs. Sometimes he was unable to impart any sacred essence to his work, and he found it lacking in ideas and inspiration; at other times his spirit rose to the occasion and he worked vigorously. Eight, nine, ten, eleven months, and the *Requiem* wasn't finished. He redoubled his efforts, forgetting his classes and his friends. He made endless revisions of the piece, but now, one way or another, he intended to finish it. Fifteen, eight, five days . . . the morning of the anniversary came and found him still at work.

He had to content himself with a simple low mass, which he attended alone. It's hard to say whether all the tears that crept stealthily into his eyes were the husband's, or if some of them were the composer's. The fact is, he never touched the *Requiem* again.

"What's the use?" he said to himself.

Still another year passed by. In the early days of 1879, his publisher appeared.

"It's been two years since we've heard anything from you," he said. "Everybody's asking if you've lost your talent. What have you been doing with yourself?"

"Nothing."

"I can understand what a blow it must have been for you, but two years have passed now. I've come to offer you a contract: twenty polkas in the next twelve months at the old price, with a larger percentage on the sales. Then we can renew after the year's over."

Pestana made a gesture of acquiescence. He had few students and had sold his house to pay his debts—daily necessities consumed his balance, which was reduced to almost nothing. He accepted the contract.

"But the first polka has to be done right away," explained the publisher. "It's urgent. Have you seen the Emperor's letter to Caxias? The liberals were summoned to power, and they're going to carry out an electoral reform. The polka will be called *Bravo for the Timely Election!* It's not political, just a good title for the occasion."

Pestana composed the first work of the contract. Despite his long period of silence, he had lost neither his originality nor his inspiration. The work carried the usual stamp of his genius. The other polkas appeared with regularity. He had saved the composers' portraits and repertories, but he avoided spending every night at the piano, to escape the temptation to experiment. Given his position of prominence, he could ask for a free ticket whenever there was a good opera or a concert. He went, tucked himself away in an inconspicuous corner, and enjoyed that world of things that would never come to flower in his mind. Once in a while, when he returned home filled with music, the unpublished maestro in him would become aroused—he would then take a seat at the piano and, with nothing specific in mind, play until he went to bed, twenty or thirty minutes later.

Thus the years passed by, until 1885. Pestana's success brought him fame, and he was finally ranked the leading composer of polkas in Rio, but the first place in town didn't satisfy this Caesar, who would have preferred even the hundredth place in Rome. He had the same mixed feelings about his compositions that he had had before, with the difference that they were now less violent. He was neither enthusiastic after the first hours nor horrified after the first week: he experienced some pleasure and a kind of ennui.

That was the year he contracted a little fever, which went up after a few days and finally became a serious matter. His life was already in danger when his publisher, who knew nothing of his illness, appeared—he had come to tell Pestana about the conservatives' rise to power and to ask him for a new polka for the occasion. The sick man's attendant, a destitute theater clarinetist, informed him of Pestana's condition. The publisher decided he shouldn't mention the new polka, but Pestana insisted on knowing why he had come. His publisher complied.

"But only after you've completely recovered," he concluded.

"As soon as my fever goes down a little," said Pestana.

A short pause followed. The clarinetist tiptoed out to prepare a medicine. The publisher stood up and got ready to leave.

"Good-by."

"Look," said Pestana, "since it's quite likely that I'm going to die any day now, I'll make you two polkas right away—the other can be used when the liberals come to power again."

It was the only joke he cracked in his entire life, and it was high time, because he died at five minutes past four the following morning, at peace with mankind and at war with himself.

MARIANA

CHAPTER 1

"I wonder what has become of Mariana," Evaristo asked himself in Carioca Square, as he took leave of an old friend who had made him remember that old sweetheart of his.

It was 1890. Evaristo had returned from Europe only days before, after an eighteen-year absence. He had left Rio de Janeiro in 1872, expecting to linger in Europe until 1874 or 1875 after seeing a few celebrated or quaint cities, but the traveler proposes and Paris disposes. Once he had entered that world, in 1873, Evaristo allowed himself to stay beyond his planned limits. He postponed his return trip for a year, then another, and at last he no longer thought of returning. He ceased to take an interest in things Brazilian—lately he had not even read the Brazilian newspapers. His only exposure to news from his homeland came from a poor Bahian student, who borrowed newspapers from him and referred occasional items of interest to him. Suddenly, in November 1889, a Parisian reporter entered his home, spoke to him of the revolution in Rio, and requested political, social, and biographical data. Evaristo reflected.

"My good man," he said to the reporter, "I think it would be better if I went myself to look for that information."

Since he had no political opinions, belonged to no political party, and had no close relatives or interests in Rio (all his concerns were in Europe), Evaristo's sudden decision seems inadequately explained by curiosity alone, but, in truth, there was no other reason. He simply wanted to see how things had changed. He inquired about the date of a premiere at the Odéon Theater, a play by a friend of his, and he figured that by leaving on the first ship and returning on the fourth one he would be back in Paris in time to buy his ticket and attend the performance. He packed his bags, hastened to Bordeaux, and embarked.

"I wonder what has become of Mariana," he now repeated, as he went down Assembléia Street. "Perhaps she's dead . . . if she's still alive, she'll surely have changed. She must be around forty-five by now . . . Whoops! Forty-eight, she was about five years younger than I. Forty-eight . . . beautiful lady! Wonderful lady! What a love we had!"

He wanted to see her. He inquired discreetly and found out she was still alive and still resided in the same house on Engenho Velho Street. However, she had not appeared for several months because of her husband, who was ill, seemingly near death.

"She too must have aged considerably," said Evaristo to the acquaintance providing him with this information.

"Good Lord, no. The last time I saw her, I thought she looked very youthful—not a day over forty! . . . You know, there are still some magnificent rosebushes around here, but there aren't any more cedars like those elegant ones we knew when we were young."

"Yes, there are, but you have to go up to Lebanon[1] to see them," retorted Evaristo.

His desire to see Mariana had increased. What feelings would they have for each other? What visions from the past would come to transform the present reality? The object of Evaristo's trip, it should be known, was not to seek pleasure but to satisfy his curiosity. Now that time had done its work, how would the two of them be affected by the memories of 1872, that sorrowful year of the separation that nearly drove him mad and nearly left her dead?

1. The cedars of Lebanon are said to become more handsome with age.—Trans.

CHAPTER 2

A few days later, he was stepping down from a carriage at Mariana's door and was handing a visiting card to the servant who opened the parlor door for him.

While he waited, he scanned the room and was amazed at what he saw. The furniture was the same set which had been there eighteen years before. His memory, incapable of reconstructing it in his absence, recognized all the pieces as well as their arrangement, which had not changed either. Everything had a time-worn appearance. Even the artificial flowers, in a huge vase on top of a buffet, had fallen apart with age. Everything was a confusion of scattered bones that one's imagination could bundle back together to restore a figure lacking only a soul.

But the soul was not lacking. Hanging on the wall above the settee was a portrait of Mariana. It had been painted when she was twenty-five. The frame, gold-leafed only once, was peeling in certain spots—it provided a contrast to her laughing, fresh figure. Time had not deteriorated her beauty. Mariana was there, dressed in the fashion of 1865, with the charming round eyes of a woman in love. It was the only living spirit in the room, but by itself it sufficed to give an atmosphere of fleeting youth to the decrepitude. Evaristo was greatly astonished. There was a chair facing the portrait. He sat down on it and gazed at the girl from another time. The painted eyes stared back at the natural eyes, perhaps surprised by the encounter and the change, since the natural eyes did not have the warmth and charm of those in the portrait. But the difference did not last long: the man's past outwardly restored his youth, and both pairs of eyes were absorbed in each other and in all their old sins.

Then, ever so slowly, Mariana descended from the canvas and the frame and sat down across from Evaristo. She bent over, extended her arms across her knees, and offered her hands to him. Evaristo in turn offered her his, and the four hands clasped affectionately. Neither one asked about anything that referred to the past, because there was no past. Both were in the present—time had stopped so instantaneously and fixedly that it seemed to have rehearsed the previous evening for this one and only, endless performance. All the clocks in the city and around the world discreetly broke their springs, and all watchmakers changed their occupations. Adieu, vieux lac de Lamartine![2] Evaristo and Mariana had anchored themselves in the ocean of time. And there came the gentlest words ever uttered by the lips of man or woman, as well as the most ardent

2. "Le Lac" ("The Lake"), a poem by Alphonse de Lamartine (1790–1869), in which he confesses all the suffering caused by the death of Elvira, his lover.—Trans.

ones, muted, rash, and whispered ones, those of jealousy and those of forgiveness.

"Have you been well?"

"Yes, and you?"

"How I suffered because of you! I've been waiting an hour for you, so anxious, nearly in tears, but you can see very well that I'm cheerful and happy, all because the most wonderful man in the world has entered the room. What kept you so long?"

"I had two interruptions on the way, and the second was much more formidable than the first."

"If you really loved me, you would have spent two minutes with both of them and would have been here forty-five minutes ago. Why are you laughing that way?"

"The second interruption was your husband."

Mariana was taken aback.

"It was here, close by," continued Evaristo. "We spoke about you, he first—I don't know what for—and he spoke with kindness, almost tenderness. I became convinced it was all a scheme, a way of gaining my confidence. At last we parted, but I stayed here watching, waiting to see if he would return. I saw no one. That is the reason for my delay, there you have the cause of all my torments."

"Don't come to me again with that eternal distrust of yours," interrupted Mariana, smiling as the portrait had done moments before. "What do you expect me to do? Xavier is my husband—I'm not going to send him away, punish him, or kill him simply because you and I love each other."

"I'm not asking you to murder him, but you do love him, Mariana."

"I love no one but you," she responded, thus avoiding a negative reply, which would have been too blunt.

That is what Evaristo thought, but he did not accept the refinement of the indirect reply. Only the cruel and simple negative would content him.

"You do love him," he insisted.

Mariana paused for an instant.

"Why must you stir up my soul and my past?" she said. "For us, the world began four months ago and will never end—or will end only when you grow tired of me, for I shall never change . . ."

Evaristo knelt, drew her arms toward him, kissed her hands, and covered his face with them. At last, he let his head rest on her knees. They remained in that position for a few moments, and then Mariana felt moisture on her fingers, raised Evaristo's head, and saw his eyes brimming with tears. What was wrong?

"Nothing," he insisted. "Good-by."

"But what happened?! What is it?"

"You love him," responded Evaristo, "and that idea terrifies and hurts me at the same time, because I am capable of killing him if I find out for certain that you still love him."

"You're a singular man," replied Mariana, after drying his eyes with her hair, which she quickly let down, providing him with the most wonderful handkerchief in the world. "You believe I love him? No, I don't love him anymore—there you have your answer. But now you must permit me to tell you everything, because my nature does not allow half confidences."

This time it was Evaristo who was shaken, but curiosity was gnawing at his heart in such a way that there was no longer any reason to be afraid—all he had to do was wait and listen. As he rested, leaning on her knees, he heard the brief story. Mariana told him about her marriage, her father's opposition, her mother's suffering, her and Xavier's perseverance. They waited ten months, firm in their decision, she less patient than he, because the passion that overcame her gave her all the force necessary for violent decisions. What tears she had shed for him! What curses came from her heart against her parents and were stifled, for she feared God and did not wish those words, as weapons of parricide, to condemn her to, worse than hell, eternal separation from the man she loved. Constancy won, time disarmed her parents, and the marriage took place after seven years had passed. The lovers' passion continued in the years following their marriage. When time brought calm, it also brought respect. Their hearts were harmonious, and the memories of their struggle were bittersweet. Serene happiness seated itself at their door like a sentinel. But the sentinel left hurriedly. In his place he left neither misfortune nor even tedium, but apathy instead—a pale, motionless figure which barely smiled and remembered nothing. It was during this time that Evaristo appeared before Mariana's eyes and enraptured her. He had not taken her out of Xavier's arms, and for this reason Evaristo was not part of the past: the past was a mystery that was likely to bring regrets.

"Regrets?" he interrupted.

"You may have assumed I did have them, but I do not, nor will I ever have any."

"Thank you!" said Evaristo after a few moments. "I appreciate your confession. I won't mention the matter again. You don't love him, that's what counts. How beautiful you are when you swear to me that way and talk about our future! Yes, we can forget about the past, now I'm here and you're free to love me!"

"Only you, my dear."

"Only me? Once more, swear to me that it's true!"

"I'll swear by these eyes," she responded, kissing his eyes, "by these lips," she continued, planting a kiss on his lips. "By my life and yours, I swear that I love only you!"

Evaristo repeated the same phrases with the same ceremonies. Then he seated himself in front of Mariana, in the same position he was in at the beginning of their meeting. She went to kneel at his feet, her arms on his knees. The locks of hair she had let down framed her face so perfectly that he regretted he wasn't a genius who could copy and bequeath it to the rest of the world. He told her this, but the young woman didn't say a word—her eyes were raised toward him, pleading. Evaristo leaned forward, gazing at her, and the two of them remained facing each other for one, two, three hours, until someone came in and interrupted them.

"Please come in."

CHAPTER 3

Evaristo was startled. He was facing a man, the same servant who had taken his visiting card. He stood up hurriedly. Mariana returned to the canvas hanging on the wall, where he saw her once more, dressed in the fashion of 1865, well coiffured and composed. As is typical of dreams, time had passed in a peculiar manner: although to Evaristo it seemed that three hours had gone by, everything had actually happened within five or six minutes, the time the servant had spent taking Evaristo's card and bringing the invitation. Meanwhile, it is certain that Evaristo still felt the sensation of the young woman's caresses, for time had even allowed him to experience his three-hour vision between the years of 1869 and 1872. The entire story came back to him with his jealousy of Xavier, his own expressions of forgiveness, and Mariana's reciprocal displays of affection. The only thing lacking was the final crisis, when Mariana's mother, aware of everything, angrily interceded and separated the two. Mariana decided to die and brought herself to drink poison—her mother's desperation was necessary to restore her to life. Xavier, then in the province of Rio, never found out about that tragedy, except that his wife had escaped death after having taken the wrong medications. Evaristo had wished to see her before he departed for Europe, but it was impossible.

"Let's go," he said to the servant, who was waiting for him.

Xavier was in the adjoining room, lying down on a settee, his wife and a few visitors at his side. Evaristo entered, full of anxiety. The light was dim, the silence profound. Mariana clutched one of the sick man's hands, watching him closely, fearing either death or a crisis. She could barely raise her eyes toward Evaristo and give him her hand—she turned all her attention toward her husband, whose face bore evidence of long suffering and whose breathing sounded like a voice out of the invisible choir. Evaristo, who had only seen Mariana's face, retired to a corner, without daring to look at her figure or even to follow her movements. The physician arrived, examined the sick man, recommended the medicines already prescribed, and left with the understanding that he would return in the evening. Mariana accompanied him to the door, questioning him in a low voice, attempting to read in his expression the words his lips refused to pronounce. It was only then that Evaristo saw her clearly. The pain seemed to have worn her down more than the years had. He then recognized the distinct quality about her figure: she did not descend from the canvas as the Mariana of his imagination had done, but from time. Before she resumed her vigil at her husband's bedside, Evaristo understood that he should be on his way, and he moved toward the door.

"Please excuse me . . . I'm very sorry I cannot speak to your husband now."

"It isn't possible, at least not now: the doctor recommended rest and quiet. Perhaps another day . . ."

"I would have come to see him before, but it was only recently that I found out . . . and I arrived from Europe only a short while ago."

"Thank you for your visit."

Evaristo extended his hand to her and left, crestfallen, and she once again sat down next to the ailing man. Neither Mariana's hand nor her eyes had revealed any particular reaction to Evaristo, and they had parted as if they were two strangers. Certainly, their love had ended long ago, her heart had grown older with time, and her husband was dying, but, he reflected, how could one explain that after eighteen years apart, Mariana had seen before her the man who had once been such an important part of her life, without the least feeling of shock, fluster, or uneasiness? There was a definite mystery. He called it a mystery. Even now, on parting, he had sensed a tightening, something that made each word a stumbling block that upset all ideas, even the simple, banal formulas of sorrow and hope. She, however, did not react to him with even the slightest trace of emotion. And as he recalled the portrait in the salon, Evaristo concluded that art was superior to nature—the canvas had retained the body and the soul. All this was crowned with an acrid twinge of resentment.

Xavier lasted another week. On his second visit to Mariana's home, Evaristo was present at the invalid's death and could not escape the natural confusion of the moment, place, and circumstances. Mariana, exhausted by her vigil and her tears, lay disheveled at the foot of the bed. When Xavier finally expired after prolonged agony, the weeping of relatives and friends was barely noticeable—Mariana's piercing scream and her subsequent loss of consciousness made her the center of attention. She was unconscious for several minutes. Once revived, she ran to the body and embraced it, sobbing in desperation and calling out the most tender names of endearment. The corpse's eyes had not been closed, and because of this a very frightening, melancholy incident occurred. After repeatedly kissing the body's eyes, Mariana apparently suffered a hallucination and cried out that her husband was still alive, that he had recovered. Despite all efforts to tear her away from the body, she would not give way—she pushed everyone aside, crying out that they wanted to take her husband away from her. She was prostrated by this new crisis and was hastily taken to another room.

When the funeral procession left the house the following day, Mariana was not present, despite her insistence on bidding farewell to her husband—she no longer possessed the strength to carry out her desire to attend the funeral. Evaristo accompanied the cortege. As he followed the funeral carriage, he barely comprehended where he was and what he was doing. At the cemetery he spoke with one of Xavier's relatives, confiding to him his sympathy for Mariana.

"It is obvious that they were very much in love," he concluded.

"Ah, very much so," said the relative. "It was a love match. I didn't attend the wedding ceremony because I didn't come to Rio until 1874. However, I found them as devoted to one another as if they were still sweethearts, and I have witnessed their life together until now. They lived for each other—I don't know if she'll last much longer in this world."

"1874," thought Evaristo, "two years afterward."

Mariana did not attend the seventh-day mass: a relative—the same one Evaristo had spoken to at the cemetery—represented her on that occasion. Evaristo discovered through him that the widow's state of health would not permit her to endanger herself by attending the commemoration of the catastrophe. He allowed a few days to pass before going to call on her to pay his last respects, but after presenting his card, he was told she was receiving no one. He then went to São Paulo, returned to Rio five or six weeks later, and prepared to leave the country. Before leaving, he still considered visiting Mariana—not so much out of courtesy, but so he might take with him the image, albeit deteriorated, of the passion of those four years.

He did not find her at home. He left, angry and disgusted, considering his action impertinent and in poor taste. A short distance away, he noticed a woman in mourning who resembled Mariana, emerging from the Church of the Holy Ghost. It was indeed Mariana, she was on foot. As she passed by the carriage, she glanced toward him, pretended not to recognize him, and continued walking—thus Evaristo's greeting was left unacknowledged. He wanted to order the coach to stop so he could say good-by to her, right there in the street, at that very moment, one minute, three words. However, as he hesitated in his decision, the coach did not stop until it had already passed the church, and by then Mariana was a considerable distance ahead. Nevertheless, he stepped out of the carriage and walked back down the street, but either out of respect or spite, he changed his mind, reentered the coach, and departed.

"Three times sincere," he concluded about her after several minutes of thought.

Less than a month later, he was in Paris. He had not forgotten his friend's new play, the premiere of which he had expected to attend at the Odéon Theater. He hastened to find out how it had fared—it had fallen flat.

"Such is the theater," Evaristo consoled the author. "There are works that fail. There are others that run forever."

A CANARY'S IDEAS

A man by the name of Macedo, who had a fancy for ornithology, related to some friends an incident so extraordinary that no one took him seriously. Some came to believe he had lost his mind. Here is a summary of his narration.

At the beginning of last month, as I was walking down the street, a carriage darted past me and nearly knocked me to the ground. I escaped by quickly side-stepping into a secondhand shop. Neither the racket of the horse and carriage nor my entrance stirred the proprietor, dozing in a folding chair at the back of the shop. He was a man of shabby appearance: his beard was the color of dirty straw, and his head was covered by a tattered cap which probably had not found a buyer. One could not guess that there was any story behind him, as there could have been behind some of the objects he sold, nor could one sense in him that austere, disillusioned sadness inherent in the objects which were remnants of past lives.

The shop was dark and crowded with the sort of old, bent, broken, tarnished, rusted articles ordinarily found in secondhand shops, and everything was in that state of semidisorder befitting such an establishment. This assortment of articles, though banal, was interesting. Pots without lids, lids without pots, buttons, shoes, locks, a black skirt, straw hats, fur hats, picture frames, binoculars, dress coats, a fencing foil, a stuffed dog, a pair of slippers, gloves, nondescript vases, epaulets, a velvet satchel, two hatracks, a slingshot, a thermometer, chairs, a lithographed portrait by the late Sisson, a backgammon board, two wire masks for some future Carnival—all this and more, which I either did not see or do not remember, filled the shop in the area around the door, propped up, hung, or displayed in glass cases as old as the objects inside them. Further inside the shop were many objects of similar appearance. Predominant were the large objects—chests of drawers, chairs, and beds—some of which were stacked on top of others which were lost in the darkness.

I was about to leave, when I saw a cage hanging in the doorway. It was as old as everything else in the shop, and I expected it to be empty so it would fit in with the general appearance of desolation. However, it wasn't empty. Inside, a canary was hopping about. The bird's color, liveliness, and charm added a note of life and youth to that heap of wreckage. It was the last passenger of some wrecked ship, who had arrived in the shop as complete and happy as it had originally been. As soon as I looked at the bird, it began to hop up and down, from perch to perch, as if it meant to tell me that a ray of sunshine was frolicking in the midst of that cemetery. I'm using this image to describe the canary only because I'm speaking to rhetorical people, but the truth is that the canary thought about neither cemetery nor sun, according to what it told me later. Along with the pleasure the sight of the bird brought me, I felt indignation regarding its destiny and softly murmured these bitter words:

"What detestable owner had the nerve to rid himself of this bird for a few cents? Or what indifferent soul, not wishing to keep his late master's pet, gave it away to some child, who sold it so he could make a bet on a soccer game?"

The canary, sitting on top of its perch, trilled this reply:

"Whoever you may be, you're certainly not in your right mind. I had no detestable owner, nor was I given to any child to sell. Those are the delusions of a sick person. Go and get yourself cured, my friend . . ."

"What?" I interrupted, not having had time to become astonished. "So your master didn't sell you to this shop? It wasn't misery or laziness that brought you, like a ray of sunshine, to this cemetery?"

"I don't know what you mean by 'sunshine' or 'cemetery.' If the canaries you've seen use the first of those names, so much the better, because it sounds pretty, but really, I'm sure you're confused."

"Excuse me, but you couldn't have come here by chance, all alone. Has your master always been that man sitting over there?"

"What master? That man over there is my servant. He gives me food and water every day, so regularly that if I were to pay him for his services, it would be no small sum, but canaries don't pay their servants. In fact, since the world belongs to canaries, it would be extravagant for them to pay for what is already in the world."

Astonished by these answers, I didn't know what to marvel at more—the language or the ideas. The language, even though it entered my ears as human speech, was uttered by the bird in the form of charming trills. I looked all around me so I could determine if I were awake and saw that the street was the same, and the shop was the same dark, sad, musty place. The canary, moving from side to side, was waiting for me to speak. I then asked if it were lonely for the infinite blue space . . .

"But, my dear man," trilled the canary, "what does 'infinite blue space' mean?"

"But, pardon me, what do you think of this world? What is the world to you?"

"The world," retorted the canary, with a certain professorial air, "is a secondhand shop with a small rectangular bamboo cage hanging from a nail. The canary is lord of the cage it lives in and the shop that surrounds it. Beyond that, everything is illusion and deception."

With this, the old man woke up and approached me, dragging his feet. He asked me if I wanted to buy the canary. I asked if he had acquired it in the same way he had acquired the rest of the objects he sold and learned that he had bought it from a barber, along with a set of razors.

"The razors are in very good condition," he said.

"I only want the canary."

I paid for it, ordered a huge, circular cage of wood and wire, and had it placed on the veranda of my house so the bird could see the garden, the fountain, and a bit of blue sky.

It was my intention to do a lengthy study of this phenomenon, without saying anything to anyone until I could astound the world with my extraordinary discovery. I began by alphabetizing the canary's language in order to study its structure, its relation to music, the bird's appreciation of aesthetics, its ideas and recollections. When this philological and psychological analysis was done, I entered specifically into the study of canaries: their origin, their early history, the geology and flora of the Canary Islands, the bird's knowledge of navigation, and so forth. We conversed for hours while I took notes, and it waited, hopped about, and trilled.

As I have no family other than two servants, I ordered them not to interrupt me, even to deliver a letter or an urgent telegram or to inform me of an important visitor. Since they both knew about my scientific pursuits, they found my orders perfectly natural and did not suspect that the canary and I understood each other.

Needless to say, I slept little, woke up two or three times each night, wandered about aimlessly, and felt feverish. Finally, I returned to my work in order to reread, add, and emend. I corrected more than one observation, either because I had misunderstood something or because the bird had not expressed it clearly. The definition of the world was one of these. Three weeks after the canary's entrance into my home, I asked it to repeat to me its definition of the world.

"The world," it answered, "is a sufficiently broad garden with a fountain in the middle, flowers, shrubbery, some grass, clear air, and a bit of blue up above. The canary, lord of the world, lives in a spacious cage, white and circular, from which it looks out on the rest of the world. Everything else is illusion and deception."

The language of my treatise also suffered some modifications, and I saw that certain conclusions which had seemed simple were actually presumptuous. I still could not write the paper I was to send to the National Museum, the Historical Institute, and the German universities, not due to a lack of material but because I first had to put together all my observations and test their validity. During the last few days, I neither left the house, answered letters, nor wanted to hear from friends or relatives. The canary was everything to me. One of the servants had the job of cleaning the bird's cage and giving it food and water every morning. The bird said nothing to him, as if it knew the man was completely lacking in scientific background. Besides, the service was no more than cursory, as the servant was not a bird lover.

One Saturday I awoke ill, my head and back aching. The doctor ordered complete rest. I was suffering from an excess of studying and was not to read or even think, nor was I even to know what was going on in the city or the rest of the outside world. I remained in this condition for five days. On the sixth day I got up, and only then did I find out that the canary, while under the servant's care, had flown out of its cage. My first impulse was to strangle the servant—I was choking with indignation and collapsed into my chair, speechless and bewildered. The guilty man defended himself, swearing he had been careful, but the wily bird had nevertheless managed to escape.

"But didn't you search for it?"

"Yes, I did, sir. First it flew up to the roof, and I followed it. It flew to a tree, and then who knows where it hid itself? I've been asking around since yesterday. I asked the neighbors and the local farmers, but no one has seen the bird."

I suffered immensely. Fortunately, the fatigue left me within a few hours, and I was soon able to go out to the veranda and the garden. There was no sign of the canary. I ran everywhere, making inquiries and posting announcements, all to no avail. I had already gathered my notes together to write my paper, even though it would be disjointed and incomplete, when I happened to visit a friend who had one of the largest and most beautiful estates on the outskirts of town. We were taking a stroll before dinner when this question was trilled to me:

"Greetings, Senhor Macedo, where have you been since you disappeared?"

It was the canary, perched on the branch of a tree. You can imagine how I reacted and what I said to the bird. My friend presumed I was mad, but the opinions of friends are of no importance to me. I spoke tenderly to the canary and asked it to come home and continue our conversations in that world of ours, composed of a garden, a fountain, a veranda, and a white circular cage.

"What garden? What fountain?"

"The world, my dear bird."

"What world? I see you haven't lost any of your annoying professorial habits. The world," it solemnly concluded, "is an infinite blue space, with the sun up above."

Indignant, I replied that if I were to believe what it said, the world could be anything—it had even been a secondhand shop . . .

"A secondhand shop?" it trilled to its heart's content. "But is there really such a thing as a secondhand shop?"

PYLADES AND ORESTES

Quintanilha begat Gonçalves. Such was the impression given by the two of them when they were together, though it wasn't because they resembled one another. On the contrary, Quintanilha's face was round, Goncalves' long—the former was short and dark, the latter tall and fair. Indeed, the picture of the two men together was a combination of totally dissimilar features. It should be added that they were about the same age. The idea of a blood relationship between the two came about because of Quintanilha's attitude toward Gonçalves—a father would have been no less devoted to a son in his thoughts, affection, and concern.

They had studied together, lived together, and taken their law degrees in the same year. Quintanilha, rather than pursuing a legal or a judiciary career, became involved in politics. Yet after serving his term as a member of the Chamber of Deputies, he abandoned his career, for he had inherited an uncle's estate, which brought him nearly thirty thousand dollars. He went to visit his friend Gonçalves, who was practicing law in Rio de Janeiro.

Although he was young, well-off, and had a close friend, it cannot be said that Quintanilha was entirely happy, as you will see. I will set aside the unhappiness his inheritance brought him in the form of his relatives' hostility, a hostility so great he was ready to give up his inheritance, until his friend Gonçalves persuaded him that such a decision would be outright madness.

"It's not your fault that you were more deserving than the others. You weren't the one who wrote the will, nor did you play up to your uncle as they did. If he left you everything it's because he thought you were more deserving than they were. Keep the money, it was your uncle's wish. Don't be a fool."

In the end Quintanilha was convinced. A few of his relatives attempted to make amends, but he refused to see them after Gonçalves had exposed their ulterior motives. One of the relatives, seeing that Quintanilha was in league with his former classmate, made his thoughts known to everyone: "Now he's done it! Just let him get involved with outsiders, he'll see what will happen!"

When Quintanilha heard this, he became enraged and ran to inform Gonçalves. Gonçalves smiled, told him he was being silly, that it wasn't worthwhile to worry about such a trifling matter, and calmed him down.

"I only want one thing," Gonçalves continued, "I want us to separate so they won't say . . ."

"So they won't say *what*? Well! That will be the day, when I choose my friends according to the whims of a crowd of scoundrels!"

"Don't talk that way, Quintanilha. You're being cruel to your family."

"To hell with them! Am I to allow that handful of swindlers to decide whom I'm to associate with? No, Gonçalves, anything you wish, except that. I'm the one who chooses my friends—it's *my* heart. Or are you . . . are you annoyed with me?"

"Annoyed with you? Don't be silly."

"Well, then?"

"It's just that I don't want them to say . . ."

"You know it's not true!"

The two of them lived a life of unparalleled devotion. Quintanilha awoke, thought about his friend, had breakfast, and went to meet him. They dined together, then paid visits, went for a stroll, or ended the evening at the theater. If Gonçalves had work to do in the evening, Quintanilha helped him dutifully—he searched for law texts, annotated them, copied them, and carried them. Gonçalves easily forgot things—a message here, a letter there, shoes, cigars, papers. Quintanilha served as his memory. At times, as they watched the young ladies pass by on Ouvidor Street, Gonçalves remembered some documents he had left in his office. Quintanilha ran to fetch them and returned so content that one could not tell whether the papers he clutched were legal documents or the grand prize in the lottery sweepstakes. All smiles and panting from exertion, he looked questioningly at Gonçalves.

"Are these the ones?"

"Let me see, yes, they are. Now give them to me."

"Never mind, I'll carry them."

At first Gonçalves sighed: "I really put you to a lot of trouble!" Quintanilha laughed at the sigh with such good humor that Gonçalves, so as not to bother him, didn't accuse himself of anything else—he complied by accepting Quintanilha's favors. With time, the favors became duties. Gonçalves said to him, "Today you'll have to remind me about this and that," and Quintanilha memorized the items or wrote them down, if there were many. Some of the reminders had to be given at specific times. It was a sight to see the kindly Quintanilha sigh with worry while he awaited this or that hour when he would have the pleasure of reminding his friend about his obligations. He brought Gonçalves letters and papers, researched answers for his correspondence, called on people, met them at the railway station, and made trips to the interior. He took it upon himself to introduce Gonçalves to good cigars, fine food, and the best entertainment. Gonçalves had only to mention a new book, or an expensive one, and a copy of it would appear on his shelf.

"You're a spendthrift," he said to Quintanilha in a reprehensive tone.

"So you think culture is a waste of money? Fine thing!" replied his friend.

At the end of the year, Quintanilha wanted the two of them to spend the holidays away from the city. Gonçalves eventually agreed, which gave Quintanilha enormous pleasure. They went up to Petrópolis. On the return trip, while they were discussing painting, Quintanilha realized that they did not have a portrait of the two of them together and arranged to have one painted. When he brought it home, his friend could not refrain from telling him it was worthless. Quintanilha was speechless.

"It's a piece of trash," insisted Gonçalves.

"But the painter told me . . ."

"You don't understand anything about painting, Quintanilha, and the painter took advantage of the occasion to swindle you. Is this a decent face? Do I have this crooked arm?"

"What a thief!"

"No, it wasn't his fault, he was only doing his job. You're the one who made this blunder, because you have no experience or feeling for art. You meant well, I'm sure."

"Yes, I did."

"And I'll bet you've already paid for the portrait."

"That's right."

Gonçalves shook his head, called him ignorant, and ended up laughing. Quintanilha, confused and annoyed, stared at the canvas for a while, then took out his pocketknife and tore it from top to bottom. As if this gesture of revenge were not enough, he returned the painting to the artist, with a note in which he transmitted to him some of the names he himself had been called and added that of ass. Life is full of such remunerations. Following this episode, a promissory note of Gonçalves'—which had been past due for days and which he was unable to pay—diverted Quintanilha's spirits. The two nearly quarreled. Gonçalves had intended to renew the note, but Quintanilha, who was the cosigner, did not believe it was worthwhile to pay interest on such a small amount of money—fifteen hundred dollars. He would lend his friend the amount due, and he could repay it when he was able. Gonçalves refused the offer and renewed the note. When it was due again, the situation was repeated, and the most Gonçalves allowed was to accept a promissory note from Quintanilha, at the same rate of interest.

"Don't you see you're humiliating me, Gonçalves? Do you mean I have to accept interest from you?"

"That, or nothing at all."

"But, my dear Gonçalves . . ."

He had to agree to it. The two were so devoted to each other that one lady called them the "newlyweds," and one man of letters, "Pylades and Orestes." They laughed about it, of course, but there was something tearful about Quintanilha's laughter, there was a moist tenderness in his eyes. Another difference between them was that Quintanilha's feeling contained a note of enthusiasm completely absent in Gonçalves', and enthusiasm cannot be invented. It is certain that Gonçalves was more likely to inspire it in Quintanilha than vice versa. Actually, Quintanilha was very sensitive to any sign of affection: a word, a glance was enough to fill him with delight. A little pat on the shoulder or belly with the intent of showing approval or accentuating their closeness was enough to make him melt with pleasure. He retold such gestures and their circumstances for two or three days afterward.

It wasn't unusual to see Quintanilha become irritated, stubborn, and abusive with others, but neither was it rare to see him laugh. At times his laughter was all-encompassing, spilling forth from his mouth, eyes, forehead, arms, and legs—his entire being became a single peal of laughter. Though not excessively sentimental, he was far from apathetic.

The debt Gonçalves owed him was to be paid in six months. On the date it was due, Quintanilha resolved not to accept payment and dined in the outskirts of the city in order to avoid his friend, lest he be asked to renew the note again. Gonçalves foiled his entire plan by bringing him the money before he was able to leave. Quintanilha's first reaction was to refuse it, telling him to keep it—for he might need it later—but the debtor insisted on paying and paid.

Quintanilha observed and greatly admired Gonçalves' perseverance in his work and zeal in his defense of his clients. Actually, Gonçalves wasn't a great lawyer, but within his limited capacities he distinguished himself.

"Why don't you get married?" Quintanilha asked him one day. "A lawyer should be married."

Gonçalves responded with laughter. He had an aunt, his only relative, whom he loved very much and who died when he was about thirty. Days later, he said to his friend: "Now you're the only one I have left."

Quintanilha felt his eyes grow moist and could not find words with which to answer. When he thought of saying "until death separates us!" it was too late. He then became twice as affectionate, and one day he awoke with the idea of making his will. Without revealing anything to Gonçalves, he named him executor and sole heir of the will.

"Keep this paper for me, Gonçalves," he said as he handed him the will. "I feel healthy, but death can come easily, and I don't want to confide my last wishes to just anyone."

Something else occurred around this time. Quintanilha had a second cousin, Camila, a modest, educated, pretty girl of twenty-two. She wasn't rich—her father, João Bastos, was a bookkeeper at a coffeehouse. He had quarreled with Quintanilha because of the inheritance, but Quintanilha attended the funeral of João Bastos' wife, and this act of kindness brought them together again. João Bastos easily forgot certain cruel names he had used when talking about Quintanilha, spoke to him kindly, and invited him to stay for dinner. Quintanilha accepted this invitation as well as others and listened to his cousin's praise of his late wife. On one occasion, when Camila left them alone, João Bastos sang the praises of his daughter, who, he affirmed, had received all her mother's moral inheritance.

"I'll never say that to her face, and don't you say a word to her. She's a modest girl, and if we begin to pay her compliments, they could go to her head. So, for example, I never tell her she's as pretty as her mother was at her age—she could become vain. But the truth is, she's prettier, don't you think? She's even got a talent for the piano, which her mother never had."

When Camila returned to the dining room, Quintanilha felt inclined to tell her everything, but he contained himself and winked at his cousin. He wanted to hear her play the piano, but she answered sadly: "Not yet, it's only been a month since mother died. Let a little more time go by. Besides, I play badly."

"Badly?"

"Very badly."

Quintanilha winked at his cousin again and hinted to the girl that the only proof of good or bad playing was to be heard at the piano. As for the period of time, it was true that it had only been a month since her mother's death. Nevertheless, it was also true that music was a natural and dignified pastime. Besides, it would suffice to play a sad piece. João Bastos approved of this viewpoint and thought of an elegiac composition. Camila shook her head.

"No, no, it wouldn't make any difference. The neighbors are likely to invent that I was playing a polka."

Quintanilha was amused and laughed. Afterward, he agreed and waited for three months to go by. During that period, he saw his cousin several times, and his last three visits were long ones separated by very brief intervals. At last he was able to hear her play the piano and was delighted. Her father confessed that at first he wasn't very fond of those German pieces, but after a while he became accustomed to them and even found them to his liking. He called his daughter "my little German girl," a nickname Quintanilha repeated in the plural: "*our* little German girl." Possessive pronouns give way to intimacy, which soon existed among the three of them—or four, counting Gonçalves, who had been introduced by his friend. But for now, let us limit ourselves to the three of them.

You have probably guessed the outcome already: Quintanilha ended up falling in love with the girl. Since Camila had a pair of wide, fatally attractive eyes, how could he have reacted in any other way? It was not that she looked at him often, and when she did, it was with the restraint of children who unwillingly obey their schoolmaster's or father's orders, but she did look at him, and her eyes inflicted fatal wounds, though unintentionally. She also smiled frequently and spoke with charm. At the piano, no matter how bored she was, she played well. In short, Camila would do nothing spontaneously, but she was no less bewitching because of it. Quintanilha discovered one morning that he had dreamed of her all night, and in the evening he realized he had thought about her all day. From this discovery he concluded that he loved her and was loved in return. He became so giddy that he was ready to have the news printed in a public announcement. At the very least, he wanted to tell Gonçalves and ran to his office. However, respect and fear made Quintanilha unable to express his feelings to his friend. Every time he opened his mouth, he swallowed his secret. He couldn't bring himself to tell Gonçalves either that day or the next. He should have told him about it before—perhaps that might have been the time to win the battle. He postponed the revelation for a week. One day he went to dinner with his friend, and after much hesitation told him everything: he loved his cousin and was loved by her.

"Do you approve, Gonçalves?"

Gonçalves grew pale, or at least grew serious: in him, seriousness was difficult to distinguish from pallor. But this time there was no doubt about it—he truly turned pale.

"Do you approve?" repeated Quintanilha.

After a few seconds, Gonçalves opened his mouth to answer, but he closed it again and fixed his eyes "on yesterday," as he said of himself when he stared off into the distance. To no avail, Quintanilha insisted that Gonçalves tell him what was wrong, what he was thinking, if he thought his love was asinine. He was so accustomed to hearing this word from Gonçalves that it no longer hurt or insulted him, even in matters so delicate and personal. Gonçalves came out of his meditation, shrugged his shoulders with a disillusioned air, and murmured these words so quietly that Quintanilha could scarcely hear them: "Don't ask me anything about it, do as you please."

"Gonçalves, what's the matter?" asked Quintanilha, as he seized his friend's hands with alarm.

Gonçalves let out a huge sigh which, had it wings, would still be in the air now. Such was Quintanilha's impression, though it was not perceived in this absurd form. The dining-room clock chimed eight, Gonçalves claimed he was going to visit a judge, and Quintanilha took his leave.

In the street, Quintanilha stopped, dumfounded. He had not understood Gonçalves' sigh, his pallor, or anything else about his friend's mysterious reaction to his news. He had entered and spoken, prepared to hear one or more of the customary epithets from Gonçalves—idiot, simpleton, dunce —but had heard none of them. On the contrary, there had been something akin to respect in Gonçalves' gestures. Quintanilha remembered nothing he had said during dinner that could have offended him: it was only after confiding to him the new feeling he had toward his cousin that his friend had become distressed.

"What could be wrong?" he thought. "What is there about Camila that wouldn't make her a good wife?"

He spent more than half an hour pondering this as he stood in front of the house. He realized Gonçalves had not left. He waited for another half hour, but there was still no sign of him. He wanted to go back inside, embrace and question him, but he lacked the nerve. In desperation, he made his way down the street and arrived at João Bastos' house. However, he was unable to see Camila, because she had retired to her room with a cold. He wanted to tell his cousin everything, for he had not yet declared his love to her. The girl's glances did not flee from his—that was all, and perhaps their relationship would not go beyond flirtation. But the moment could not have been better for clearing up the situation. By telling her what had happened between him and his friend, he would have the opportunity to let her know he loved her and was going to ask for her hand in marriage. It was one consolation amid all that agony, but fate kept her from him, and he left the house in a worse state than he was in when he entered. He returned to his house.

He didn't fall asleep until two o'clock in the morning, and even then it wasn't for rest, but for new and greater agitation. He dreamed he was crossing a long, old bridge between two mountains. Halfway across, he saw a figure rise up from below and stand firmly in front of him—it was Gonçalves. "You scoundrel!" he said, his eyes aflame. "Why have you come to take away the woman I love, who belongs to me? Here, you might as well take my whole heart." With a rapid gesture he opened his breast, tore out his heart, and thrust it into Quintanilha's mouth. Quintanilha attempted to grab hold of the friendly heart and replace it in Gonçalves' breast, but it was impossible. His jaws closed down upon it. He tried to spit it out, but the result was worse: his teeth buried themselves in the heart. He tried to speak, but his mouth was too full. Finally, Gonçalves raised his arms and extended his hands out to Quintanilha in the type of damning gesture seen in melodramas when he was young. In his eyes welled up two enormous tears which filled the valley with water. Then he flung himself downward and disappeared. Quintanilha awoke choking.

The effect of his nightmare was so vivid that he even brought his hands up to his mouth to tear out his friend's heart. He found only his tongue, rubbed his eyes, and sat up. Where was he? What had happened? What about the bridge? And Gonçalves? He regained his composure, understood what had occurred, and lay back down to endure another period of insomnia, less severe than the first: he fell asleep at four in the morning.

The following day, recalling both the dream and the real events of the night before, he arrived at the conclusion that his friend Gonçalves was his rival, loved his cousin, was perhaps loved by her . . . Yes, that could be the problem. Quintanilha suffered through two cruel hours. Finally he became calm and went to Gonçalves' office to find out once and for all if his conjectures were true.

Gonçalves was writing some arguments for an appeal. He interrupted his work to glance at Quintanilha, sat up, and opened the strongbox where he kept his important papers. He took out Quintanilha's will and handed it to him.

"What's this all about?"

"You're going to change your marital status."

Quintanilha sensed tears in Gonçalves' voice, or at least, so it seemed to him. He asked Gonçalves to keep the will, for it could be confided to no one else. He insisted, but the only response was the harsh sound of pen on paper. The pen wasn't writing well, the handwriting was shaky, the corrections were more numerous than usual, the dates were probably in error. Gonçalves consulted the law books with such melancholy that Quintanilha was saddened. At times he stopped everything, his pen and his consultations, in order to sit and stare "at yesterday."

"I understand," said Quintanilha suddenly. "She will be yours."

"She? Whom do you mean?" Gonçalves wanted to ask, but since his friend was already flying down the stairs like an arrow, he continued writing.

All the rest of the story cannot be guessed, but it will suffice to know the ending. It can neither be guessed nor believed, but the human soul is capable of great endeavors, in good as well as evil. Quintanilha wrote another will, bequeathing everything to his cousin with the condition that she marry his friend. Camila refused the bequest, but she was so moved when her cousin told her about Gonçalves' tears that she accepted both Gonçalves and his tears. For this occasion, Quintanilha could find nothing more appropriate than to write a third testament, in which he willed everything to his friend.

The end of the story was pronounced in Latin. Quintanilha served as best man for the bridegroom and was godfather to the first two children. One day in 1893, as he was bringing some candy to his godchildren, he was hit by a stray bullet while crossing the 15th of November Square and was killed almost instantly. He is buried in Saint John's Cemetery. The grave is simple, and the headstone bears an epitaph that ends with these pious words: "Pray for him!" Orestes still lives, but without the remorse of the Greek model. Pylades is now Sophocles' mute character. Pray for him!

FUNERAL MARCH

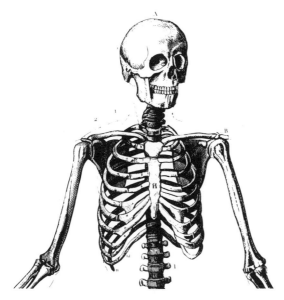

That August night in 1867, Representative Cordovil couldn't sleep a wink. He had left the Cassino Fluminense early, after the Emperor's departure, and during the dance he hadn't felt the slightest indisposition, physical or moral. On the contrary, it was an excellent evening, so excellent that one of his enemies, who had been suffering from heart trouble, passed away before ten o'clock, and the news reached the casino a little after eleven.

You will naturally conclude that Cordovil was pleased with the man's death, that his pleasure was the sort that weak and spiteful souls derive from revenge for lack of a better source. You are mistaken: rather than pleasure, he experienced a sense of relief. The death, which had been expected for months, was one of those that bites, chews, crushes, and grinds away at its victim. Cordovil was aware of the man's suffering. Some friends, to console him for past injuries he had endured, would come to tell him what they had learned about the condition of his adversary, who was confined to an armchair, living through ghastly nights, mornings without a spark of hope, and afternoons without a sign of deliverance. Cordovil responded to the messengers' tidings with words of compassion, which they adopted and repeated elsewhere. The man's suffering had finally ended—hence Cordovil's feeling of relief.

This feeling was in keeping with Cordovil's sense of compassion. Except in politics, he never wished for another's misfortune. When he got out of bed and prayed, "Our father which art in heaven, hallowed be thy name. Thy kingdom come. Thy will be done, on earth, as it is in heaven. Give us this day our daily bread. And forgive us our debts, as we forgive our debtors," he wasn't imitating a certain friend of his, who mouthed the same prayer while continuing to hold his debtors accountable. This friend went so far as to charge more than was due, that is, if he heard another being slandered, he memorized what he heard, added to it, and would then repeat it. Nevertheless, on the following day, Jesus' lovely prayer was repeated by those same lips with their habitual charity.

Cordovil didn't follow his friend's example—he truly forgave. It is conceivable that a touch of sluggishness invaded his forgiveness, but it was nothing really obvious. Sluggishness nourishes considerable virtue. A diminution of the power of evil is nothing to sneeze at. Don't forget that the representative only wished for another's misfortune in politics and that his dead enemy had been a personal enemy. I cannot say that I know the reason for their enmity, and the man's name was forgotten after he died.

"The poor man is finally at rest!" said Cordovil.

At the casino they chatted about the deceased's drawn-out illness. They also spoke about the different kinds of death in this world. Cordovil said he preferred Caesar's to all of them, not on account of the instrument used but because it was unexpected and quick.

"Tu quoque?"[1] asked a colleague, laughing.

To which Cordovil, picking up the allusion, replied: "If I had a son, I would like to die by his hand. Parricide, since it is so uncommon, would make the death more tragic."

And so it continued, all in the spirit of fun. Cordovil was sleepy when he left the dance, and despite the poorly paved streets he dozed off in his carriage. Close to home, he felt the carriage stop and heard the sound of voices. Two policemen were lifting the body of a dead man.

"Murdered?" he asked his footman, who had descended from his perch to find out what it was all about.

"I don't know, sir."

"Ask."

"That young man knows what happened," said the footman, pointing to a stranger talking to a group of people.

The youth approached the small carriage door before Cordovil could refuse to listen to his explanation, then he summarized the accident he had witnessed.

1. "Thou too?" Brutus is understood in the allusion.—Trans.

"We were walking along, he in front and I behind. I think he was whistling a polka. As he was about to cross the street over to the Mangue district, I saw him stop suddenly. I don't know exactly what happened, but his body sort of contracted, and he fell down unconscious. A doctor, who came from a little two-story house, arrived at once, examined the man, and said he'd died all of a sudden. People were gathering about, and it took the police a long time to get here. Now they've picked him up. Do you want to see the corpse?"

"No, thank you. Can we get through now?"

"Yes."

"Thanks again. Let's go, Domingos."

Domingos climbed up to his seat, the coachman started up the horses, and the carriage continued on its way to Saint Christopher Street, where Cordovil lived. As he rode, Cordovil thought about the stranger's death. Everything considered, it was a good death. Compared with that of his personal enemy, it was excellent. The man had started to whistle, contemplating God only knows what past joy or hope for the future. He was reliving what he had already lived, or foreseeing what he could yet live, when death abruptly seized the joy or hope, and the man went off to his eternal resting place. He died without pain, or if there was any it was perhaps very brief, like a flash of lightning that leaves the night darker.

Then he placed himself in the other's position. What if he had died the stranger's death in the casino? He would not have been dancing—at forty, he no longer danced. It could in fact be said that he had already given up dancing by the time he had reached his twentieth year. He wasn't a ladies' man, and he had had only one serious attachment in his lifetime. He had married when he was twenty-five, only to become a widower five weeks later. He never remarried. It's not that he lacked prospects, especially after he lost his grandfather, who left him two country estates. He sold both of them and began to live alone, made two trips to Europe, and led an active political and social life. Lately, both politics and society seemed to annoy him, but having no other way to spend his time, he didn't give them up. Once he even became Secretary of the Navy, but it only lasted for seven months. He wasn't disappointed by his dismissal: he wasn't ambitious and was more inclined to peace and quiet than to an active life.

But what if he had died suddenly in the casino, during a waltz or a quadrille, right in the center of the dance floor? It could really happen this way. Cordovil imagined the scene: he face downward or on his back, the crowd's pleasure disturbed, the dance interrupted ... maybe it wouldn't happen just like that. Perhaps some would be astonished, others a little frightened, and the men would try to console the ladies. The musicians would continue to play in the midst of the confusion, until they realized what had happened. There would be no lack of able-bodied men to carry him to a side room, already dead, completely dead.

"Just like Caesar's death," he reflected.

Then he corrected himself: "No, better than that, no threats, no weapons or blood, just a simple fall and the end. I wouldn't feel anything."

Cordovil laughed, smiled, and did whatever he could to free himself from the sensation of fear. In all truth, it would be better to die like that than after long days or months or years of suffering, like the adversary he had lost a few hours before. This wasn't even dying: it was a tip of the hat, lost in the air along with the very hand and life that had put the gesture into motion. A quick nod followed by eternal sleep. He found only one flaw in it: the showiness of it all. That death in the middle of a dance, in the presence of the Emperor, to the music of Strauss, described, discussed, and exaggerated in the newspapers, that death would seem made to order. Well, he should just be patient, as long as it happened suddenly.

He thought alternatively that it could take place in the House of Representatives the next day, at the beginning of the debate over the budget. He had the floor, now he was reeling off facts and figures. He refused to think about the matter, it wasn't worth his time—but his thoughts persisted and appeared of their own accord. The assembly room of the House instead of the casino, without ladies, or with just a few of them in the upper galleries. A vast silence. Standing, Cordovil would begin his speech, after looking around the room and acknowledging the Speaker and the President: "I beg the House to hear me out, I shall be brief, I shall try to be fair . . ." At this point a cloud would cover his eyes, his tongue would stop, and his heart too, and he would suddenly fall to the floor. The people in the House and the galleries would be astonished. Many representatives would hasten to assist him. One of them, a doctor, would confirm his death. Rather than saying it had been sudden, as the doctor who came from his two-story house on Aterrado Street had said, he would use a more technical term. After a few words from the President and the selection of a committee to accompany the deceased to the cemetery, the House would be recessed.

Cordovil wanted to laugh about his imagining the circumstances beyond his own death: the crowds of people set in motion, the funeral procession, even the obituary notices, which he quickly read and memorized. That is, he thought he wanted to laugh, but would really have preferred to doze off. His eyes, while close to home and bed, refused to concern themselves with sleep and remained wide open.

Then death, which in his imagination had already taken place at the casino, and during the plenary session of the House the following day, appeared in his carriage. He took it into his head that they would find his body when they came to open the door. He would thus depart from a clamorous night and without any kind of struggle or resistance, enter another peaceful night without conversations, dances, or meetings. A shudder that came over him made him realize that none of this had actually happened. The carriage arrived at his villa and came to a halt. Domingos jumped down from his seat to open the door. Cordovil stepped down with legs and heart alive and went through the side door, where his slave Florindo was waiting for him with a lit candle. He climbed the stairs, and his feet sensed that the steps were of this world—if they had been from the other they would have gone down, naturally. Upon entering his room he looked at his bed, in which he had enjoyed many a deep and peaceful slumber.

"Did anyone come by?"

"No, sir," replied his slave absently. But he immediately corrected himself: "Yes, someone did come, sir, that doctor who had lunch with you last Sunday."

"What did he want?"

"He told me he had come to give you some good news, and he left a note—which I put at the foot of your bed."

The note told of his enemy's death—the doctor was one of those friends who used to tell him about the progress of the dying man's illness. This happy fellow, who always gave Cordovil a warm embrace, wanted to be first to announce the outcome. The scoundrel had finally died. He didn't say it in precisely those terms, but the ones he used amounted to the same thing. He added that delivering this message had not been the object of his visit. He had come to spend the evening, and only after he arrived did he learn that Cordovil had gone to the casino. As he was about to leave, he happened to remember the other's death and asked Florindo to allow him to write a few lines. Cordovil was again reminded of his enemy's suffering, and with a sad and helpless gesture he exclaimed in a whisper: "The poor man! God bless sudden deaths!"

If Florindo had related Cordovil's anxiety to the note, he might have regretted allowing the doctor to leave it. But he wasn't thinking about that. He helped his master prepare for bed, received his last orders, and left. Cordovil lay down.

"Ah!" he sighed, stretching out his tired body.

Then he entertained the idea that he could die in his sleep. This possibility, the best of all because it would catch him already half-dead, brought in its wake a thousand fantasies that swept the sleep from his eyes. They were, in part, a repetition of the others: his speech in the House, the President's words, the selection of a committee for the funeral procession, and the rest. He heard friends and servants expressing their regrets, and read the obituaries, all of them warm and sincere. Then he began to suspect it was all a dream. It wasn't. He was awake. Now he called himself back to the room and the bed.

The nightlamp gave reality a more distinct shape. He fought off his morbid ideas and hoped that cheerful thoughts would take their place and dance before his eyes until he was tired. He tried to conquer one vision with another. He ingeniously invoked his five senses, which were keen and active, in order to summon forth people and events from the past. Through the lens of a different and remote time, he reviewed many things he had seen and done. Once again he tasted delicacies he hadn't eaten for years. His ears picked up the sounds of light and heavy footsteps, jovial and sad songs, and every utterance imaginable. All his senses were at work for a period of time which he was unable to measure.

Now he tried to sleep and closed his eyes tightly. But sleep wouldn't come, not on his back or stomach, nor on his left or right side. He got up to look at the clock: it was three A.M. Automatically he raised it to his ear to see if it had stopped. It was running, he wound it. Yes, there was still time for a sound sleep. He went back to bed, covering his head so he wouldn't see the light.

Then sleep tried to enter—silently and unobtrusively, as death would come in if it wanted to carry him off suddenly, for ever and ever. Cordovil forced his eyes shut, which was a mistake, because this effort emphasized his desire to sleep. He tried to relax them, which was the right thing to do. Sleep, about to withdraw, turned around and came to stretch out beside him, encircling him with those simultaneously light and heavy arms that completely restrict a person's movements. Cordovil felt them and tried to snuggle up to them even more with his own arms. The image isn't precise, but I don't have another at hand or time to go looking for one. I shall just reveal the result of his gesture, which was to turn sleep away by annoying that repairman of the weary.

"What could he have against me tonight?" sleep would ask, if it could speak. But silence is the very essence of sleep. When sleep seems to be talking, it is only a dream speaking—not sleep, which is stone, and even stone speaks if one strikes it, like the pavers at work on my street are doing now. Every blow on stone elicits a sound, and the regularity of the act makes the sound so punctual that it seems like clockwork. People talking in the streets, vendors' cries, carriage wheels, the sound of footsteps, none of these things I hear now gave life to Cordovil's street and night. Everything seemed conducive to sleep.

When Cordovil was finally about to doze off, the idea that he might die in his sleep returned again. Sleep backed away and fled. This state of uncertainty lasted for a long time. Whenever sleep was on the verge of closing his eyes, the thought of death opened them, until he threw the sheet back and got out of bed. He opened a window and leaned against the sill. The sky was beginning to brighten, and the indistinct shapes of workers and merchants on their way to town passed through the streets below. Cordovil felt a shiver. Not knowing whether it was cold or fear, he went to put on a calico nightshirt and then returned to the window. It must have been cold, because he stopped shivering.

People continued to go by, the sky brightened, and the station whistle signaled the departure of a train. Men and things were emerging from their resting places. The sky began to economize, turning out the stars as the sun came up to ply its trade. Everything suggested life. The thought of death naturally withdrew and completely disappeared, while Cordovil, who had longed for it in the casino, desired it the following day in the House of Representatives, and faced it in his carriage, turned his back on it when he saw it coming in with sleep, its older or younger brother—I cannot say which.

Many years later Cordovil requested and received death, not the sudden death he had hoped for but a long lingering one—the death of a slowly decanting wine. Drop by drop the wine would pass from the first bottle into the second, until the impurities were completely filtered. Now he saw the philosophy in it: only the sediment would go to the cemetery. He was never to understand the meaning of a sudden death.

WALLOW, SWINE!

One evening, many years ago, I was strolling with a friend on the terrace of the Saint Peter of Alcantara Theater between the second and third acts of *The Sentence, or Trial by Jury*. I can no longer remember details of the play, only its title, but that's precisely what led us to a discussion of the jury system and a related event I've never been able to forget.

I've always been opposed to trial by jury (said my friend). I'm not against the concept, which is liberal. My repugnance at the thought of condemning anybody is based on Scripture: "Do not judge, that you may not be judged." Nonetheless, I served on a jury on two occasions. At that time the district court was in the old Aljube district at the end of Goldsmith Street, near the Hill of the Immaculate Conception.

I had so many qualms that I voted to acquit all but two of the defendants. In fact, it never seemed to me that any of the crimes was proven beyond doubt, and a couple of the charges seemed particularly open to question. The first person I helped condemn was a clean-cut youth accused of forging a document for an insignificant sum. He didn't deny it, nor would it have been possible for him to do so. Although he admitted carrying out the deed, he said that another party, whose name he didn't mention, had suggested the possibility of forgery as a solution to his dire predicament. In a sad and subdued voice, he said that God, who could see into men's hearts, would give the real criminal his deserved punishment. His pale complexion and lifeless eyes inspired pity. The prosecuting attorney found a clear confession of guilt in the defendant's words and appearance. But the attorney for the defense showed that, quite the contrary, the accused's state of depression, distress, and paleness had been caused by the slandering of his innocent name.

I have seldom witnessed such a brilliant debate. Although the prosecutor's speech was short, it was eloquent, delivered in a tone that suggested indignation and hatred. The presentation of the defense revealed talent and was unusual in that it was the defending attorney's debut in court. The relatives, colleagues, and friends who had awaited the young man's first speech were not disappointed by his admirable defense, which would have saved his client if there had been any possibility of saving him. But the crime was as plain as the nose on your face. The lawyer died two years later, in 1865. What a loss for mankind! Believe me, I lament the death of a promising young man more than that of an older man . . . But let me get on with my story: the prosecutor gave his rebuttal and the defender rejoined. The presiding judge summarized the proceedings of the trial, which were then handed over to me, the foreman of the jury.

I won't reveal what took place in the jury room because it's secret. Besides, it's of no relevance to my story, which I confess would also be best left untold. I'll try to make it brief, as the third act is about to begin.

One of the jurors was a portly red-headed man who seemed more convinced of the defendant's guilt than the others. The proceedings were discussed and examined, and our decision was announced: eleven to one. Only the red-headed juror had been uneasy before the final decision was reached. After our vote had assured the accused's conviction, he was satisfied and said that an acquittal would have been a sign of weakness or worse. When the juror who had voted against conviction proffered a few words in defense of the youth, the redhead, whose name was Lopes, replied angrily: "What do you mean? It's a clear-cut case of guilt!"

"Let's not argue the point," I said, and the others agreed with me.

"I'm not arguing, I'm just defending my vote," continued Lopes. "The crime is more than proven. Like all defendants, he denies he's responsible, but the fact is, he committed a crime, and what a crime! And all for twenty dollars, a pittance. Let the swine grovel in his filth! Wallow, swine, wallow!"

"Wallow, swine!" I confess I was astonished. Not that I understood what he was getting at—quite the contrary, I neither understood him nor felt he was being fair, and that's why I was astonished. I finally went to the door of the jury room and knocked. When the door was opened for us, I approached the bench, handed our deliberations to the judge, and the accused was convicted. His lawyer appealed, but I don't know if the appeal was accepted or the conviction upheld. I lost sight of the matter.

When I left the courthouse, I walked along thinking about Lopes' statement and thought I grasped the meaning of it. "Wallow, swine!" was as though he had said the convicted man was the worst kind of thief—he was just a common thief. This interpretation occurred to me as I was coming down Goldsmith Street, just before I reached the corner of Saint Peter Street. I even retraced my steps for a distance to see if I could find Lopes and shake his hand, but there was no sign of him. The next day I came across our names while reading the newspaper, and his complete name was given. However, it didn't seem worth the trouble to look him up. "That's the book of life for you," my son used to say when he dabbled in verse. He also said that as the pages are turned, they are no sooner digested than neglected. Although I can't recall the verse form he used, that's how he rhymed it.

Some time thereafter, he told me in prose that I shouldn't refuse jury duty, to which I had just been summoned. I replied that I wouldn't serve and quoted Scripture to support my refusal. He insisted, saying it was a duty, a gratuitous service that no responsible citizen could deny his country. I went and sat in judgment three times.

The defendant in one of the trials was the teller at the Bank of Honest Labor, who'd been accused of embezzlement. I had heard of the case, which wasn't covered in much detail by the newspapers. I didn't actually care to read the news about crimes. When the accused appeared, he went to take his seat on the famous defendant's bench. He was a thin, red-haired man. I looked at him more carefully and shuddered, for he seemed to bear a striking resemblance to the juror who had served with me some years before. At that moment I was unable to positively identify him because he was so much thinner, but he looked like the same person, his hair and beard were the same color, and even his voice and name—Lopes—were the same.

"What is your name?" asked the presiding judge.

"Antônio do Carmo Ribeiro Lopes."

I had already forgotten the first three names, but the fourth was the same. Then other things began to confirm my suspicions, and it wasn't long before I recognized him as the very same Lopes who had been a juror several years before. As a matter of fact, I can now tell you that these circumstances prevented me from following the hearing attentively, and many things escaped me. When I came to my senses and was finally ready to listen carefully, the hearing was almost over. Lopes either firmly denied all the allegations or gave ambiguous answers that complicated the proceedings. He glanced about the courtroom without fear or anxiety, and I think I even detected a hint of a smile at the corners of his mouth.

Then the charges were read. He was accused of duplicity and the embezzlement of $110,000. I won't go into how the crime or the criminal was detected, because the orchestra is tuning up and we're running out of time. But I will say that I remember being most impressed by the inquiries, the documents, the teller's attempt to abscond, the testimony of the witnesses, and a lot of other incriminating evidence. While I was looking at Lopes, I heard people reading aloud or talking. He was listening too, but with his head held high, he looked at the court clerk, the judge, the ceiling, and the people—I among them—who were about to judge him. When he looked in my direction, he failed to recognize me. He stared at me and smiled, as he did with the others. His court manners were interpreted in different ways by the prosecution and the defense, just as the behavior of the defendant in the other trial had been interpreted years before. The prosecuting attorney saw a clear-cut case of duplicity in Lopes' manner, and the defending attorney tried to show that only innocence and the certainty of acquittal could explain his relaxed and confident demeanor.

While each lawyer presented his case, I began to consider the fateful turn of events which had placed Lopes in the same position as the young man he had once voted to convict, and I naturally repeated the scriptural precept: "Do not judge, that you may not be judged." I confess that on several occasions I felt a chill run down my spine. Not that I would have embezzled money, but what if I had killed somebody in a moment of rage or had been falsely accused of embezzlement? The same person who had once sat in judgment was now being judged by others.

As I thought about the scriptural precept, I was suddenly reminded of Lopes' "Wallow, swine!" You can't imagine how I was shaken by this thought. I recalled everything I just told you: the little speech Lopes gave in the jury room and those words, "Wallow, swine!" I saw he wasn't just a common thief—he really stole with class. It's the verb that defines the action so harshly: "Wallow, swine!" He meant that nobody should stoop so low unless the stakes are high. No one should wallow for a small sum.

Ideas and words were swimming through my head so fast that I was unable to catch the judge's summary of the proceedings. After he had finished and had read the charges, we retired to the jury room. I can tell you now that I was so certain of Lopes' embezzlement of the $110,000 that I voted for his conviction. Among the many documents was a letter written by him, which in my mind proved his guilt. But the other jurors didn't read with my eyes. Two jurors voted with me, nine denied Lopes' guilt, and he walked away a free man. The difference in the vote was so great that I began to have second thoughts. Perhaps I was mistaken. I still feel some pangs of conscience. Fortunately, if Lopes really didn't commit the crime, he wasn't convicted because of my vote. This thought offers some consolation, but the pangs still return. If you don't care to be judged by another, it's best to withhold your judgment. Wallow, swine! Let the swine roll, grovel, or wallow as they choose, but don't try to judge your fellow man. The music's stopped now. Let's return to our seats.

TRANSLATORS' NOTE

In translating the stories we used volume 2 of the Aguilar edition of Machado de Assis' complete works (*Obra Completa*, Rio: Editôra José Aguilar, Ltda., 1962). Following are the titles and dates of publication of the translated stories:

"The Bonzo's Secret" ("O Segrêdo do Bonzo," 1882)

"Those Cousins from Sapucaia" ("Primas de Sapucaia," 1883)

"Alexandrian Tale" ("Conto Alexandrino," 1883)

"The Devil's Church" ("A Igreja do Diabo," 1883)

"A Strange Thing" ("Singular Ocorrência," 1883)

"Final Chapter" ("Último Capítulo," 1883)

"A Second Life" ("A Segunda Vida," 1884)

"Dona Paula" ("D. Paula," 1884)

"The Diplomat" ("O Diplomático," 1884)

"The Companion" ("O Enfermeiro," 1884)

"Evolution" ("Evolução," 1884)

"Adam and Eve" ("Adão e Eva," 1885)

"Eternal!" ("Eterno!" 1887)

"A Celebrity" ("Um Homem Célebre," 1888)

"Mariana" ("Mariana," 1891)

"A Canary's Ideas" ("Idéias de Canário," 1895)

"Pylades and Orestes" ("Pílades e Orestes," 1903)

"Funeral March" ("Marcha Fúnebre," 1905)

"Wallow, Swine!" ("Suje-se Gordo!" 1905)

Although both translators carefully read and commented on each other's work, Jack Schmitt is primarily responsible for translating "The Bonzo's Secret," "A Strange Thing," "Dona Paula," "The Companion," "Eternal!" "A Celebrity," "Funeral March," and "Wallow, Swine!" Lorie Ishimatsu is primarily responsible for "The Devil's Church," "Those Cousins from Sapucaia," "Alexandrian Tale," "Final Chapter," "A Second Life," "The Diplomat," "Evolution," "Adam and Eve," "Mariana," "A Canary's Ideas," and "Pylades and Orestes."